Another Round of Stories by the Christmas Fire

Charles Dickens

with

Eliza Lynn Linton

George A. Sala

Adelaide Anne Procter

Elizabeth Gaskell

Edmund Saul Dixon

W.H. Wills

Samuel Sidney

William Gaskell

Edited by

Melisa Klimaszewski

ET REMOTISSIMA PROPE

Hesperus Classics

Hesperus Classics
Published by Hesperus Press Limited
4 Rickett Street, London sw6 1ru
www.hesperuspress.com

First published in *Household Words* in 1853
First published by Hesperus Press Limited, 2008

This edition edited by Melisa Klimaszewski
Introduction and notes © Melisa Klimaszewski, 2008
Foreword © Kathryn Hughes, 2008

Designed and typeset by Fraser Muggeridge studio
Printed in Jordan by Jordan National Press

isbn: 978-1-84391-186-9

CONTENTS

FOREWORD

The first thing that strikes you about *Another Round of Stories by the Christmas Fire* is just how timeless, or rather out-of-time, it all feels. The tales and poems collected in this festive spin-off from Charles Dickens' wildly popular *Household Words* are set in a pre-industrial landscape furnished with manor houses, baronets, cottages, fox hunts and wayside inns. Meanwhile, railway stations, workshops and greengrocers – the usual clutter of everyday life in 1853 – are nowhere to be seen. Nothing necessarily wrong with that, but it must have made for a strangely dislocated reading experience for the hundreds of thousands of busy town-dwellers who made up the magazine's core audience.

What makes this disjuncture all the more remarkable is that, just ten years previously, it was Dickens himself who had scored a massive cultural and commercial hit by imagining a new kind of Christmas for the modern age. In *A Christmas Carol* (1843) he shows how, despite the tendency for human relationships to buckle under capitalism, it is still possible to heal those bonds without recourse to a change of scene. At the end of the Carol we remain in a recognisably modern London, one with counting houses, dingy courts and cramped lodgings. The main units of social organisation are still the nuclear family and the office. Moreover, the 'Victorian Christmas' which developed in the lea of Dickens' iconic text was remarkable for its up-to-the-minute ingredients. The tree famously arrived with Prince Albert from Germany in 1840, the turkey turned up from America in the 1860s, and the Christmas card was devised by the time-pressed bureaucrat Henry Cole as a way of avoiding the chore of writing personal seasonal greetings to every member of his social network.

So, ten years on from the determined modernity of *A Christmas Carol*, it is intriguing to see how the contributors to *Another Round* have chosen, quite independently of one another, to interpret their brief, which was to produce a tale which, while seasonal in feel, should not labour the point. Just as the first generation of mass-produced Christmas cards insisted on showing coaching inns and pheasants rather than steam trains and turkeys, so the England depicted here by authors including Elizabeth Gaskell, George Sala, and Charles Dickens himself, is determinedly nostalgic.

Most obviously, there's the insistence that these stories are spoken yarns, told around a seasonal fire, rather than components of a mass-produced printed text. Commissioned around the time of the Equinox, and published at the Solstice, *Another Round* (in fact there had been only one before) presents itself as part of an ancient tradition of celebrating the dying year rather than a shrewd commercial intervention in the publishing market. (If this last point seems harsh, it is worth recalling that in 1847, the first year since *A Christmas Carol* in which he failed to produce a December book, Dickens admitted that, quite apart from not wanting to disappoint the reading nation, he was 'very loath to lose the money'.)

Striking too is the way in which all these pieces draw heavily upon traditional literary models, particularly the ghost, folk and fairy tale. Dickens' opening piece, 'The Schoolboy's Story', sets the tone with a spectacular reversal of fortune in which an impoverished young schoolmaster is raised to overnight riches by a surprise bequest. The next piece, Eliza Lynn Linton's haunting 'The Old Lady's Story', takes place between two Halloweens. George Sala's 'Over The Way's Story', meanwhile, self-consciously plays with elements of both 'Beauty and the Beast' and 'Cinderella', while in 'Uncle

George's Story' a bride plans to marry in a lace gown 'valuable and handsome enough for a princess'. What's more, in this fairy tale landscape the gaping rifts between rags and riches, this world and the next, can be breached by love alone. Thus in Adelaide Procter's poem 'The Angel's Story', the child who has been cosseted in luxury is reunited with the ragged boy who once stood gaping at his glittering gates. In 'The Schoolboy's Story', Jane, a maid recruited from a charity (just one step up from the workhouse), is raised to the status of a lady as a reward for her years of patient support for the impoverished schoolmaster. More seriously, but no less incongruously, the narrator of Eliza Lynn Linton's ghost story is saved from the evil machinations of her spectral suitor by the sacrificial love of a saintly sister.

Also conspicuous are the economic activities in which the main characters are engaged. Or perhaps *not* engaged would be more accurate. With the exception of Sala's John Simcox, who is employed as a Cheapside clerk – exactly the sort of work that readers of *Household Words* would be familiar with – all the men described here enjoy independent means. We meet a baronet, a squire, and several gentleman farmers. Admittedly, there's also a highwayman and a smuggler – but these are archetypes which belong firmly to an imaginary eighteenth century rather than the here-and-now of high Victorianism. The younger heroes, too, display none of that spirit of economic and social adventure we're familiar with from contemporary novels. In 'Uncle George's Story', a young bridegroom lives in a cottage which has been done up fabulously thanks to his father's bottomless wealth. Meanwhile, in 'The Colonel's Story' the hero delays the tediousness of a post in the East India Company by becoming 'carver, cellar keeper, and secretary' – in other words, a kind of dependant gentleman servant – to his wealthy uncle.

What does it all mean? Were Dickens' contributors caught up in a regressive fantasy in which they found comfort in imagining themselves as ladies and gentlemen of leisure, released from the tyranny of publishers' deadlines? It's a beguiling thought, but an unlikely one. By this point, Elizabeth Gaskell had already published *Mary Barton* and *North and South*, and she continued to be deeply engaged in exploring conditions in the modern industrial city. Eliza Lynn Linton's forty-year writing career likewise demonstrated an acute alertness to contemporary culture. Her most celebrated work included a scandalously frank book on sexual double standards and a thundering condemnation of fashionable young womanhood, the much-quoted 'The Girl of the Period'. George Sala, one of the most prominent journalists of the day, earned (and lost) a fortune by producing articles, stories and novels which spoke directly to the experiences and desires of a new mass-market readership. In short, the contributors to *Another Round* chose to mark Christmas by telling stories which emphasised the unchanging nature of things because this, they knew, was what their readers wanted.

All of which suggests that by 1853 Christmas had begun to take on many of the 'traditional' qualities with which we still associate it today. Dickens' earlier attempt to create a new kind of seasonal narrative for the modern age had been overtaken, just a decade later, by a wave of desire for something which seemed older, unbroken. As economic conditions eased, and the 'hungry forties' gave way to the sunnier 'fifties' and the triumph of the Great Exhibition, it began to seem safe once more to pillage England's past for images and tropes which could be used to stress the continuity rather than the rupture of recent years. Earlier commentators such as Scott and Southey had been keen to heal what they perceived as the social anomie of the new industrial age by reviving an older, feudal idea of Christmas. According to this model the semi-mythical 'Baron's Hall' became the venue for a period of feasting which extended from mid December until Twelfth Night. Christmas Day itself – the focus of so much anxiety and anticipation in *A Christmas Carol* – was downplayed in favour of a whole seasonal stretch during which high and low, master and servant, supped together and even, for a while, changed places in the subversive figure of 'The Lord of Misrule'. Stories, too, were exchanged around a communal fire, cementing allegiances which were rooted in kith networks rather than the contractual agreements which marked modern labour relations.

It is a delightful picture, if an historically inaccurate one. Still, it helps to explain the more puzzling aspects of *Another Round of Stories by the Christmas Fire*. In their determination to set their pieces in the unlocated past (only Elizabeth Gaskell gives a precise year for her story – the rest stay deliberately vague), the contributors sought to legitimise the new Victorian Christmas by providing it with an instant pedigree. Without exactly saying so – everyone took Dickens at his word and steered clear of too many specific seasonal references – these writers grafted the one or two day Christian holiday of the mid 1850s onto a much longer midwinter tradition of celebrating social harmony. With the Chartist terrors of the 1840s now receding, it was becoming increasingly clear that industrial Britain would survive the nineteenth century without descending into revolutionary terror. What better way of explaining and promoting this remarkable stability – the envy of all Europe – than by emphasising the social and cultural continuities between the Christmases of 'once upon a time' and 'now'?

– *Kathryn Hughes, 2008*

INTRODUCTION

In early September 1853, Charles Dickens wrote to his friend
Angela Burdett-Coutts, 'It is dark now, and raining hard –
good suitable circumstances in which to devise a Christmas
number, which is my present employment.' Had Dickens
himself written the chilling stories of seductive ghosts,
child murders, and violent crimes that appear in the year's
Christmas number, we might understand why the gloomy
atmosphere he described seemed so 'suitable'. But the story
with which he opens the 1853 number is downright cheerful,
and the most disturbing tales come from the pens of others.
The narrative variety evident in *Another Round of Stories
by the Christmas Fire* shows Dickens continuing to develop
his talents as craftsman of a most fascinating Victorian
collaborative form.

Beginning in 1850, Dickens issued a special number of
his weekly journal, *Household Words*, to celebrate the holiday
season each December. These Christmas numbers were so
successful that, regardless of his constant work as a novelist, editor, and highly sought after celebrity figure, Dickens
produced them for eighteen years straight. He solicited
contributions from colleagues and friends, added them to his
own tales, then arranged the number to his satisfaction. The
year 1852 marked the first time that Dickens began to develop
a frame concept to organise the pieces. *A Round of Stories
by the Christmas Fire* (1852) positioned speakers, listeners,
writers, and readers alike around a single metaphorical
fireside. Dickens was so pleased with the effect that he told
Elizabeth Gaskell in a letter from 13th April 1853 that he had
already decided to continue the next number 'on the plan
of the last'.

By creating a second *Round of Stories*, Dickens invoked the familiar elements of the previous year, instantly positioning the new Christmas number as part of a tradition, while also pledging fresh stories for his readers' entertainment. Second only to Dickens himself, Samuel Sidney provided the most continuity between years, for his work had appeared in each of the three preceding Christmas numbers (although Sidney continued to write for *Household Words*, this would be his last Christmas issue). The voices of Edmund Saul Dixon and Elizabeth Gaskell also carry over from the first to the second *Round*. George A. Sala as well as W.H. (William Henry) Wills, the sub-editor of *Household Words*, had each written for at least one previous Christmas number. Eliza Lynn and Adelaide Anne Procter were the only new Christmas contributors, but since they had both placed pieces in weekly issues of the periodical, Dickens was not dealing with unknown writers. The invitations he extended to his colleagues were warm, and he was eager to see what they would produce.

As with the previous Christmas numbers, Dickens' was the only name to appear in print. For all of the weekly issues of *Household Words*, Dickens called himself the periodical's 'Conductor' and, with a few exceptions for serialised novels, included no individual bylines for authors. It was not unusual for Victorian writers to sacrifice bylines so that periodicals could work toward creating a unified voice, but some authors did complain about the practice. Dickens' unique conducting metaphor at once acknowledges and subordinates other creative talents.

Perhaps more remarkable than Dickens collecting so many distinct voices in a single text are the multiple layers of collaboration in this number. One contributor, W.H. Wills, was crucial to the early and continued success of *Household*

Words; he was responsible for managing the office, corresponding with all contributors, and editing pieces to meet Dickens' consistently exacting expectations. 'Uncle George's Story' showcases Wills' creative presence at the journal, as he collaborates so completely with Edmund Saul Dixon that their voices seamlessly merge in a tale of young lovers and hidden smuggling tunnels. Elizabeth and William Gaskell's collaboration is more disjointed; she wrote the introductory paragraphs to the verse, and he translated the ballad from Théodore Hersart de La Villemarqué's (1815–95) *Barzaz-Breiz* (1839), which purported to record ancient Breton oral tradition. In 'The Scholar's Story', then, we have William Gaskell's English translation of Villemarqué's French translation of an ancient Breton folk ballad, and the introductory paragraph tells us that the 'scholar' heard the story from the mother of the woman who told it to Villemarqué. The multiple filtrations and overlapping voices of this story are seemingly endless. That it was Elizabeth Gaskell (rather than Dickens) who weaved it all into the frame concept further exemplifies Dickens' capacity to cede control of the narrative voice. Indeed, he nearly begged Elizabeth Gaskell to contribute in 1853, despite the fact that she had refused to follow Dickens' suggestions for altering the conclusion of her piece in the first *Round*.

While Dickens was generally pleased with the finished products once the numbers were complete, and he certainly delighted in the positive reception that greeted the early Christmas numbers, there are signs that he did remain nervous about the collaborations. In 'The Schoolboy's Story', the speaker abruptly instructs the reader, 'Don't look at the next storyteller, for there's more yet.' A schoolboy might understandably be unsure of his ability to hold the attention of the adults at the fireside, but this address also indicates that

Dickens may have felt insecure about holding his readers' attention. This direct address reminds readers to visualise the fireside and actually prepares them for the pending change in voice, but it does so in a self-conscious manner that also creates a defensive atmosphere. Eliza Lynn Linton's 'Old Lady' seems poised to encroach on the narrative space of Dickens' young boy.

George A. Sala's 'Over the Way's Story' confirms that Dickens may have had good reason to be anxious about just how such a juxtaposition of voices would affect his own. Barnard Braddlescroggs in Sala's tale of a transformed grouch clearly riffs on more than Scrooge's name from Dickens' wildly popular *A Christmas Carol* (1843). For Braddlescroggs, transformation occurs over a span of several years rather than in a confused night of time travelling with spirits, and a young girl whose patient duty to an alcoholic father threatens her health takes the place of an uncomplaining disabled boy. The result for both protagonists is an excessive and buoyant generosity. Without bylines to identify authors, but with the common knowledge that Dickens 'conducted' his contributors, readers could legitimately read this piece in any number of ways: as self-parody, friendly parody on the part of a contributor, laudatory imitation by Sala, or Dickens unoriginally repeating his own storylines.

The narrators of *Another Round of Stories by the Christmas Fire* range from the mundane to the extraordinary, from the generic 'Old Lady' to the more specific 'Uncle George'. The first *Round*'s 'Somebody's Story' finds a counterpart in *Another Round*'s 'Nobody's Story'. This structure places a celestial 'Angel' on the same footing as a very earthly 'Colonel', suggesting that narrators and listeners alike should feel free to cross boundaries of all sorts, and the stories' themes are as varied as their tellers. Tales of abusive parents and life-shattering seductions appear alongside traditional ghost stories and recollections of happy romances. Dickens draws upon his own childhood experiences to recount school-house pranks in the lively and humorous 'Schoolboy's Story'. Other tales are good reminders of just how disturbing many Victorian Christmas narratives were. 'The Scholar's Story' is shockingly horrific in its account of the bloody and senseless murders of animals, an infant, and a young wife. The angel of Procter's 'The Angel's Story' is actually an agent of death who takes the life of a generous boy as a means of 'mercy' before 'sin and the hard world' can 'defile' him, but the boy has already shown himself to be compassionate and kind even when surrounded by wealth and haughty servants. The angel's appearance seems to suggest that humanity's sin is too strong for even the most righteous children to withstand – a rather pessimistic world view. An imperialist British spirit, in the form of offensive tropes and troublesome portraits of non-English figures, also pervades the number, although 'The Colonel's Story' is the only title directly alluding to imperial ventures.

Dickens was in the midst of his own travels when he wrote his pieces for this number. 'The Schoolboy's Story' was composed in Rome, 'Nobody's Story' in Venice. For the first time, Dickens used his own stories as bookends for the number. R.H. (Richard Henry) Horne's pieces conclude the first two Christmas numbers, and Eliza Griffiths' poem marks the end of the first *Round*. Following *Another Round*, Dickens would continue the practice of using his own work to start and finish the next two special issues. Although the frame concepts he devised continued to sound fairly straightforward, Dickens' conducting became increasingly complicated, and controlling the tone of the beginning and end of this number seemed to increase his comfort in granting contributors significant leeway with the themes of their pieces. Writing to Elizabeth Gaskell on 19th September 1853, he clearly states that any story for the number '...need *not* be about Xmas and winter, and it need *not* have a moral...'. Dickens is emphatic in his instructions, stressing that no single theme or message need emerge, perhaps because he knew he could use his own tales to provide enough moralising in the way of holiday spirit for all.

Indeed, the closing words of *Another Round of Stories by the Christmas Fire* are unusual in echoing the direct address to readers of the first story. Speaking of the poor, Dickens' final narrator implores, 'O! Let us think of them this year at the Christmas fire, and not forget them when it is burnt out.' Wherever the other stories of the *Round* might have taken readers' imaginations, Dickens takes back the narrative reins with a strong call for social responsibility. Acknowledging that this year's fire will fade, he leaves readers energised with compassion and curious about what form the Christmas fire, and its attendant stories, will take when next rekindled.

– *Melisa Klimaszewski, 2008*

Another Round of Stories by the Christmas Fire

Being the Extra Christmas Number
Of Household Words

Conducted By Charles Dickens

Containing The Amount Of
One Regular Number And A Half

Christmas, 1853

THE SCHOOLBOY'S STORY
[by Charles Dickens]

Being rather young at present – I am getting on in years, but still I am rather young – I have no particular adventures of my own to fall back upon. It wouldn't much interest anybody here, I suppose, to know what a screw the Reverend is, or what a griffin *she* is, or how they do stick it into parents – particularly hair cutting, and medical attendance. One of our fellows was charged in his half's account twelve and sixpence for two pills – tolerably profitable at six and threepence apiece, I should think – and he never took them either, but put them up the sleeve of his jacket.

As to the beef, it's shameful. It's *not* beef. Regular beef isn't veins. You can chew regular beef. Besides which, there's gravy to regular beef, and you never see a drop to ours. Another of our fellows went home ill, and heard the family doctor tell his father that he couldn't account for his complaint unless it was the beer. Of course it was the beer, and well it might be!

However, beef and old Cheeseman are two different things. So is beer. It was Old Cheeseman I meant to tell about; not the manner in which our fellows get their constitutions destroyed for the sake of profit.

Why, look at the piecrust alone. There's no flakiness in it. It's solid – like damp lead. Then our fellows get nightmares, and are bolstered for calling out and waking other fellows. Who can wonder!

Old Cheeseman one night walked in his sleep, put his hat on over his nightcap, got hold of a fishing rod and a cricket bat, and went down into the parlour, where they naturally thought from his appearance he was a Ghost. Why, he never would have done that, if his meals had been wholesome.

When we all begin to walk in our sleeps, I suppose they'll be sorry for it.

Old Cheeseman wasn't second Latin Master then; he was a fellow himself. He was first brought there, very small, in a post-chaise, by a woman who was always taking snuff and shaking him – and that was the most he remembered about it. He never went home for the holidays. His accounts (he never learnt any extras) were sent to a Bank, and the Bank paid them; and he had a brown suit twice a year, and went into boots at twelve. They were always too big for him, too.

In the Midsummer holidays, some of our fellows who lived within walking distance, used to come back and climb the trees outside the playground wall, on purpose to look at Old Cheeseman reading there by himself. He was always as mild as the tea – and *that's* pretty mild, I should hope! – so when they whistled to him, he looked up and nodded; and when they said 'Halloa Old Cheeseman, what have you had for dinner?' he said 'Boiled mutton;' and when they said 'An't it solitary, Old Cheeseman?' he said 'It is a little dull, sometimes;' and then they said 'Well, goodbye, Old Cheeseman!' and climbed down again. Of course it was imposing on Old Cheeseman to give him nothing but boiled mutton through a whole Vacation, but that was just like the system. When they didn't give him boiled mutton they gave him rice pudding, pretending it was a treat. And saved the butcher.

So Old Cheeseman went on. The holidays brought him into other trouble besides the loneliness; because when the fellows began to come back, not wanting to, he was always glad to see them: which was aggravating when they were not at all glad to see him, and so he got his head knocked against walls, and that was the way his nose bled. But he was a favourite in general. Once, a subscription was raised for him; and, to keep up his spirits, he was presented before the holidays with two white mice, a rabbit, a pigeon, and a beautiful puppy. Old Cheeseman cried about it – especially soon afterwards, when they all ate one another.

Of course Old Cheeseman used to be called by the names of all sorts of cheeses – Double Glo'sterman, Family Cheshireman, Dutchman, North Wiltshireman, and all that. But he never minded it. And I don't mean to say he was old in point of years – because he wasn't – only he was called, from the first, Old Cheeseman.

At last, Old Cheeseman was made second Latin Master. He was brought in one morning at the beginning of a new half, and presented to the school in that capacity as 'Mr Cheeseman'. Then our fellows all agreed that Old Cheeseman was a spy, and a deserter, who had gone over to the enemy's camp, and sold himself for gold. It was no excuse for him that he had sold himself for very little gold – two pound ten a quarter, and his washing, as was reported. It was decided by a Parliament which sat about it, that Old Cheeseman's mercenary motives could alone be taken into account, and that he had 'coined our blood for drachmas'. The Parliament took the expression out of the quarrel scene between Brutus and Cassius.[1]

When it was settled in this strong way that Old Cheeseman was a tremendous traitor, who had wormed himself into our fellows' secrets on purpose to get himself into favour by giving up everything he knew, all courageous fellows were invited to come forward and enrol themselves in a Society for making a set against him. The President of the Society was First boy, named Bob Tarter. His father was in the West Indies, and he owned, himself, that his father was worth Millions. He had great power among our fellows, and he wrote a parody, beginning,

'Who made believe to be so meek

That we could hardly hear him speak,

Yet turned out an Informing Sneak?

Old Cheeseman.'[2]

– and on in that way through more than a dozen verses, which he used to go and sing, every morning, close by the new master's desk. He trained one of the low boys too, a rosy-cheeked little Brass who didn't care what he did, to go up to him with his Latin Grammar one morning, and say it so: – *Nominativus pronominum* – Old Cheeseman, *raro exprimitur* – was never suspected, *nisi distinctionis* – of being an informer, *aut emphasis gratiá* until he proved one. *Ut* – for instance, *Vos damnastis* – when he sold the boys. *Quasi* – as though, *dicat* – he should say, *Pretærea nemo* – I'm a Judas![3] All this produced a great effect on Old Cheeseman. He had never had much hair; but what he had, began to get thinner and thinner every day. He grew paler and more worn; and sometimes of an evening he was seen sitting at his desk with a precious long snuff to his candle, and his hands before his face, crying. But no member of the Society could pity him, even if he felt inclined, because the President said it was Old Cheeseman's conscience.

So Old Cheeseman went on, and didn't he lead a miserable life! Of course the Reverend turned up his nose at him, and of course *she* did – because both of them always do that, at all the masters – but he suffered from the fellows most, and he suffered from them constantly. He never told about it, that the Society could find out; but he got no credit for that, because the President said it was Old Cheeseman's cowardice.

He had only one friend in the world, and that one was almost as powerless as he was, for it was only Jane. Jane was a sort of a wardrobe woman to our fellows, and took care of the boxes. She had come at first, I believe, as a kind of apprentice –

some of our fellows say from a Charity, but *I* don't know – and after her time was out, had stopped at so much a year. So little a year, perhaps I ought to say, for it is far more likely. However, she had put some pounds in the Savings' Bank, and she was a very nice young woman. She was not quite pretty; but she had a very frank, honest, bright face, and all our fellows were fond of her. She was uncommonly neat and cheerful, and uncommonly comfortable and kind. And if anything was the matter with a fellow's mother, he always went and showed the letter to Jane.

Jane was Old Cheeseman's friend. The more the Society went against him, the more Jane stood by him. She used to give him a good-humoured look out of her stillroom⁴ window, sometimes, that seemed to set him up for the day. She used to pass out of the orchard and the kitchen garden (always kept locked, I believe you!) through the playground, when she might have gone the other way, only to give a turn of her head, as much as to say 'Keep up your spirits!' to Old Cheeseman. His slip of a room was so fresh and orderly, that it was well known who looked after it while he was at his desk; and when our fellows saw a smoking hot dumpling on his plate at dinner, they knew with indignation who had sent it up.

Under these circumstances, the Society resolved, after a quantity of meeting and debating, that Jane should be requested to cut Old Cheeseman dead; and that if she refused, she must be sent to Coventry⁵ herself. So a deputation, headed by the President, was appointed to wait on Jane, and inform her of the vote the Society had been under the painful necessity of passing. She was very much respected for all her good qualities, and there was a story about her having once waylaid the Reverend in his own study and got a fellow off from severe punishment, of her own kind comfortable heart.

So the deputation didn't much like the job. However they went up, and the President told Jane all about it. Upon which Jane turned very red, burst into tears, informed the President and the deputation, in a way not at all like her usual way, that they were a parcel of malicious young savages, and turned the whole respected body out of the room. Consequently it was entered in the Society's book (kept in astronomical cypher for fear of detection), that all communication with Jane was interdicted; and the President addressed the members on this convincing instance of Old Cheeseman's undermining.

But Jane was as true to Old Cheeseman as Old Cheeseman was false to our fellows – in their opinion at all events – and steadily continued to be his only friend. It was a great exasperation to the Society, because Jane was as much a loss to them as she was a gain to him; and being more inveterate against him than ever, they treated him worse than ever. At last, one morning, his desk stood empty, his room was peeped into and found to be vacant, and a whisper went about among the pale faces of our fellows that Old Cheeseman, unable to bear it any longer, had got up early and drowned himself.

The mysterious looks of the other masters after breakfast, and the evident fact that Old Cheeseman was not expected, confirmed the Society in this opinion. Some began to discuss whether the President was liable to hanging or only transportation for life, and the President's face showed a great anxiety to know which. However, he said that a jury of his country should find him game; and that in his address he should put it to them to lay their hands upon their hearts, and say whether they as Britons approved of Informers, and how they thought they would like it themselves. Some of the Society considered that he had better run away until he found a Forest, where he might change clothes with a woodcutter and stain his face with blackberries; but the majority believed that if he stood his ground, his father – belonging as he did to the West Indies, and being worth Millions – could buy him off.

All our fellows' hearts beat fast when the Reverend came in, and made a sort of a Roman, or a Field Marshal, of himself with the ruler; as he always did before delivering an address. But their fears were nothing to their astonishment when he came out with the story that Old Cheeseman, 'so long our respected friend and fellow pilgrim in the pleasant plains of knowledge,' he called him – O yes! I dare say! Much of that! – was the orphan child of a disinherited young lady who had married against her father's wish, and whose young husband had died, and who had died of sorrow herself, and whose unfortunate baby (Old Cheeseman) had been brought up at the cost of a grandfather who would never consent to see it, baby, boy, or man: which grandfather was now dead, and serve him right – that's *my* putting in – and which grandfather's large property, there being no will, was now, and all of a sudden and for ever, Old Cheeseman's! Our so long respected friend and fellow pilgrim in the pleasant plains of knowledge, the Reverend wound up a lot of bothering quotations by saying, would 'come among us once more' that day fortnight, when he desired to take leave of us himself in a more particular manner. With these words, he stared severely round at our fellows, and went solemnly out.

There was precious consternation among the members of the Society, now. Lots of them wanted to resign, and lots more began to try to make out that they had never belonged to it. However, the President stuck up, and said that they must stand or fall together, and that if a breach was made it should be over his body – which was meant to encourage the Society: but it didn't. The President further said, he would consider the position in which they stood, and would give them his best opinion and advice in a few days. This was eagerly looked for, as he knew a good deal of the world on account of his father's being in the West Indies.

After days and days of hard thinking, and drawing armies all over his slate, the President called our fellows together, and made the matter clear. He said it was plain that when Old Cheeseman came on the appointed day, his first revenge would be to impeach the Society, and have it flogged all round. After witnessing with joy the torture of his enemies, and gloating over the cries which agony would extort from them, the probability was that he would invite the Reverend, on pretence of conversation, into a private room – say the parlour into which Parents were shown, where the two great globes were which were never used – and would there reproach him with the various frauds and oppressions he had endured at his hands. At the close of his observations he would make a signal to a Prizefighter concealed in the passage, who would then appear and pitch into the Reverend till he was left insensible. Old Cheeseman would then make Jane a present of from five to ten pounds, and would leave the establishment in fiendish triumph.

The President explained that against the parlour part, or the Jane part, of these arrangements he had nothing to say; but, on the part of the Society, he counselled deadly resistance. With this view he recommended that all available desks should be filled with stones, and that the first word of the complaint should be the signal to every fellow to let fly at Old Cheeseman. The bold advice put the Society in better spirits, and was unanimously taken. A post about Old Cheeseman's size was put up in the playground, and all our fellows practised at it till it was dinted all over.

When the day came, and Places were called, every fellow sat down in a tremble. There had been much discussing and disputing as to how Old Cheeseman would come; but it was the general opinion that he would appear in a sort of a triumphal car drawn by four horses, with two livery servants in front, and the Prizefighter in disguise up behind. So, all our fellows sat listening for the sound of wheels. But no wheels were heard, for Old Cheeseman walked after all, and came into the school without any preparation. Pretty much as he used to be, only dressed in black.

'Gentlemen,' said the Reverend, presenting him, 'our so long respected friend and fellow pilgrim in the pleasant plains of knowledge, is desirous to offer a word or two. Attention, gentlemen, one and all!'

Every fellow stole his hand into his desk and looked at the President. The President was all ready, and taking aim at Old Cheeseman with his eyes.

What did Old Cheeseman then, but walk up to his old desk, look round him with a queer smile as if there was a tear in his eye, and begin in a quavering mild voice, 'My dear companions and old friends!'

Every fellow's hand came out of his desk, and the President suddenly began to cry.

'My dear companions and old friends,' said Old Cheeseman, 'you have heard of my good fortune. I have passed so many years under this roof – my entire life so far, I may say – that I hope you have been glad to hear of it for my sake. I could never enjoy it without exchanging con-gratulations with you. If we have ever misunderstood one another at all, pray my dear boys let us forgive and forget. I have a great tenderness for you, and I am sure you return it. I want in the fulness of a grateful heart to shake hands with you every one. I have come back to do it, if you please, my dear boys.'

Since the President had begun to cry, several other fellows had broken out here and there: but now, when Old Cheeseman began with him as first boy, laid his left hand affectionately on his shoulder and gave him his right; and when the President said 'Indeed I don't deserve it, Sir; upon my honour I don't;' there was sobbing and crying all over the school. Every other fellow said he didn't deserve it, much in the same way; but Old Cheeseman, not minding that a bit, went cheerfully round to every boy, and wound up with every master – finishing off the Reverend last.

Then a snivelling little chap in a corner, who was always under some punishment or other, set up a shrill cry of 'Success to Old Cheeseman! Hoorray!' The Reverend glared upon him, and said '*Mr* Cheeseman, Sir.' But, Old Cheeseman protesting that he liked his old name a great deal better than his new one, all our fellows took up the cry; and, for I don't know how many minutes, there was a thundering of feet and hands, and such a roaring of Old Cheeseman, as never was heard.

After that, there was a spread in the dining room of the most magnificent kind. Fowls, tongues, preserves, fruits, confectionaries, jellies, neguses, barley – sugar temples, trifles, crackers – eat all you can and pocket what you like – all at Old Cheeseman's expense. After that, speeches, whole holiday, double and treble sets of all manners of things for all manners of games, donkeys, pony chaises and drive yourself, dinner for all the masters at the Seven Bells (twenty pound a head our fellows estimated it at), an annual holiday and feast fixed for that day every year, and another on Old Cheeseman's birthday – Reverend bound down before the fellows to allow it, so that he could never back out – all at Old Cheeseman's expense.

And didn't our fellows go down in a body and cheer outside the Seven Bells? O no!

But there's something else besides. Don't look at the next storyteller, for there's more yet. Next day, it was resolved that the Society should make it up with Jane, and then be dissolved. What do you think of Jane being gone, though! 'What? Gone for ever?' said our fellows, with long faces. 'Yes, to be sure,' was all the answer they could get. None of the people about the house would say anything more. At length, the first boy took upon himself to ask the Reverend whether our old friend Jane was really gone? The Reverend (he has got a daughter at home – turn-up nose, and red) replied severely, 'Yes Sir, Miss Pitt is gone.' The idea of calling Jane, Miss Pitt! Some said she had been sent away in disgrace for taking money from Old Cheeseman; others said she had gone into Old Cheeseman's service at a rise of ten pounds a year. All that our fellows knew, was, she was gone.

It was two or three months afterwards, when, one afternoon, an open carriage stopped at the cricket field, just outside bounds, with a lady and gentleman in it, who looked at the game a long time and stood up to see it played. Nobody thought much about them, until the same little snivelling chap came in, against all rules, from the post where he was Scout, and said, 'It's Jane!' Both Elevens forgot the game directly, and ran crowding round the carriage. It *was* Jane! In such a bonnet! And if you'll believe me, Jane was married to Old Cheeseman.

It soon became quite a regular thing when our fellows were hard at it in the playground, to see a carriage at the low part of the wall where it joins the high part, and a lady and gentleman standing up in it, looking over. The gentleman was always Old Cheeseman, and the lady was always Jane.

The first time I ever saw them, I saw them in that way. There had been a good many changes among our fellows then, and it had turned out that Bob Tarter's father wasn't worth Millions! He wasn't worth anything. Bob had gone for a soldier, and Old Cheeseman had purchased his discharge. But that's not the carriage. The carriage stopped, and all our fellows stopped as soon as it was seen.

'So you have never sent me to Coventry after all!' said the lady, laughing, as our fellows swarmed up the wall to shake hands with her. 'Are you never going to do it?'

'Never! never! never!' on all sides.

I didn't understand what she meant then, but of course I do now. I was very much pleased with her face though, and with her good way, and I couldn't help looking at her – and at him too – with all our fellows clustering so joyfully about them.

They soon took notice of me as a new boy, so I thought I might as well swarm up the wall myself, and shake hands with them as the rest did. I was quite as glad to see them as the rest were, and was quite as familiar with them in a moment.

'Only a fortnight now,' said Old Cheeseman, 'to the holidays. Who stops? Anybody?'

A good many fingers pointed at me, and a good many voices cried, 'He does!' For it was the year when you were all away; and rather low I was about it, I can tell you.

'Oh!' said Old Cheeseman. 'But it's solitary here in the holiday time. He had better come to us.'

So I went to their delightful house, and was as happy as I could possibly be. They understand how to conduct themselves towards boys, *they* do. When they take a boy to the play, for instance, they *do* take him. They don't go in after it's begun, or come out before it's over. They know how to bring a boy up, too. Look at their own! Though he is very little as yet, what a capital boy he is! Why, my next favourite to Mrs Cheeseman and Old Cheeseman, is young Cheeseman.

So, now I have told you all I know about Old Cheeseman. And it's not much after all, I am afraid. Is it?

THE OLD LADY'S STORY
[by Eliza Lynn Linton]

I have never told you my secret, my dear nieces. However, this Christmas, which may well be the last to an old woman, I will give the whole story; for though it is a strange story, and a sad one, it is true; and what sin there was in it I trust I may have expiated by my tears and my repentance. Perhaps the last expiation of all is this painful confession.

We were very young at the time, Lucy and I, and the neighbours said we were pretty. So we were, I believe, though entirely different; for Lucy was quiet, and fair, and I was full of life and spirits; wild beyond any power of control, and reckless. I was the elder by two years; but more fit to be in leading-strings myself than to guide or govern my sister. But she was so good, so quiet, and so wise, that she needed no one's guidance; for if advice was to be given, it was she who gave it, not I; and I never knew her judgment or perception fail. She was the darling of the house. My mother had died soon after Lucy was born. A picture in the dining room of her, in spite of all the difference of dress, was exactly like Lucy; and, as Lucy was now seventeen and my mother had been only eighteen when it was taken, there was no discrepancy of years.

One Allhallow's Eve a party of us – all young girls, not one of us twenty years of age – were trying our fortunes round the drawing room fire; throwing nuts into the brightest blaze, to hear if mythic 'He's loved any of us, and in what proportion; or pouring hot lead into water, to find cradles and rings, or purses and coffins; or breaking the whites of eggs into tumblers half full of water, and then drawing up the white into pictures of the future – the prettiest experiment of all.[6] I remember Lucy could only make a recumbent figure of hers, like a marble monument

17

in miniature; and I, a maze of masks and skulls and things that looked like dancing apes or imps, and vapoury lines that did not require much imagination to fashion into ghosts or spirits; for they were clearly human in the outline, but thin and vapoury. And we all laughed a great deal, and teazed one another, and were as full of fun and mischief, and innocence and thoughtlessness, as a nest of young birds.

There was a certain room at the other end of our rambling old manor house, which was said to be haunted, and which my father had therefore discontinued as a dwelling room, so that we children might not be frightened by foolish servants; and he had made it into a lumber place – a kind of ground-floor granary – where no one had any business. Well, it was proposed that one of us should go into this room alone, lock the door, stand before a glass, pare and eat an apple very deliberately, looking fixedly in the glass all the time; and then, if the mind never once wandered, the future husband would be clearly shown in the glass. As I was always the foolhardy girl of every party, and was, moreover, very desirous of seeing that apocryphal individual, my future husband (whose non-appearance I used to wonder at and bewail in secret), I was glad enough to make the trial, notwithstanding the entreaties of some of the more timid. Lucy, above all, clung to me, and besought me earnestly not to go – at last, almost with tears. But my pride of courage, and my curiosity, and a certain nameless feeling of attraction, were too strong for me. I laughed Lucy and her abettors into silence; uttered half a dozen bravados; and, taking up a bedroom candle, passed through the long silent passages, to the cold, dark, deserted room – my heart beating with excitement, my foolish head dizzy with hope and faith. The church clock chimed a quarter past twelve as I opened the door.

It was an awful night. The windows shook, as if every instant they would burst in with some strong man's hand on the bars, and his shoulder against the frames; and the trees howled and shrieked, as if each branch were sentient and in pain. The ivy beat against the window, sometimes with fury, and sometimes with the leaves slowly scraping against the glass, and drawing out long shrill sounds, like spirits crying to each other. In the room itself it was worse. Rats had made it their refuge for many years, and they rushed behind the wainscot and down inside the walls, bringing with them showers of lime and dust, which rattled like chains, or sounded like men's feet hurrying to and fro; and every now and then a cry broke through the room, one could not tell from where or from what, but a cry, distinct and human; heavy blows seemed to be struck on the floor, which cracked like parting ice beneath my feet, and loud knockings shook the walls. Yet in this tumult, I was not afraid. I reasoned on each new sound very calmly – and said, 'Those are rats,' or 'those are leaves,' and 'birds in the chimney,' or 'owls in the ivy,' as each new howl or scream struck my ear. And I was not in the least frightened or disturbed; it all seemed natural and familiar. I placed the candle on a table in the midst of the room, where an old broken mirror stood; and, looking steadily into the glass (having first wiped off the dust), I began to eat Eve's forbidden fruit, wishing intently, as I had been bidden, for the apparition of my future husband.

In about ten minutes I heard a dull, vague, unearthly sound; felt, not heard. It was as if countless wings rushed by, and small low voices whispering too; as if a crowd, a multitude of life was about me; as if shadowy faces crushed up against me, and eyes and hands, and sneering lips, all mocked me. I was suffocated. The air was so heavy – so filled with life, that I could not breathe. I was pressed on from all sides, and could not turn nor move without parting thickening vapours. I heard my own name – I can swear to that today! I heard it repeated through the room; and then bursts of laughter followed, and the wings rustled and fluttered, and the whispering voices mocked and chattered, and the heavy air, so filled with life, hung heavier and thicker, and the Things pressed up to me closer, and checked the breath on my lips with the clammy breath from theirs.

I was not alarmed. I was not excited; but I was fascinated and spellbound; yet with every sense seeming to possess ten times its natural power. I still went on looking in the glass – still earnestly desiring an apparition – when suddenly I saw a man's face peering over my shoulder in the glass. Girls, I could draw that face to this hour! The low forehead, with the short curling hair, black as jet, growing down in a sharp point; the dark eyes, beneath thick eyebrows, burning with a peculiar light; the nose and the dilating nostrils; the thin lips, curled into a smile – I see them all plainly before me now. And – O, the smile that it was! – the mockery and sneer, the derision, the sarcasm, the contempt, the victory that were in it! – even then it struck into me a sense of submission. The eyes looked full into mine: those eyes and mine fastened on each other; and, as I ended my task, the church clock chimed the half-hour; and, suddenly released, as if from a spell, I turned round, expecting to see a living man standing beside me. But I met only the chill air coming in from the loose window, and the solitude of the dark night. The Life had gone; the wings had rushed away; the voices had died out, and I was alone; with the rats behind the wainscot, the owls hooting in the ivy, and the wind howling through the trees.

Convinced that either some trick had been played me, or that someone was concealed in the room, I searched every corner of it. I lifted lids of boxes filled with the dust of ages and with rotting paper lying like bleaching skin. I took down the chimney-board, and soot and ashes flew up in clouds. I opened dim old closets, where all manner of foul insects had made their homes, and where daylight had not entered for generations: but I found nothing. Satisfied that nothing human was in the room, and that no one could have been there tonight – nor for many months, if not years – and still nerved to a state of desperate courage, I went back to the drawing room. But, as I left that room I felt that something flowed out with me; and, all through the long passages, I retained the sensation that this something was behind me. My steps were heavy; the consciousness of pursuit having paralysed, not quickened me; for I knew that when I left that haunted room I had not left it alone. As I opened the drawing room door – the blazing fire and the strong lamplight bursting out upon me with a peculiar expression of cheerfulness and welcome – I heard a laugh close at my elbow, and felt a hot blast across my neck. I started back, but the laugh died away, and all I saw were two points of light, fiery and flaming, that somehow fashioned themselves into eyes beneath their heavy brows, and looked at me meaningly through the darkness.

They all wanted to know what I had seen; but I refused to say a word; not liking to tell a falsehood then, and not liking to expose myself to ridicule. For I felt that what I had seen was true, and that no sophistry and no argument, no reasoning and no ridicule, could shake my belief in it. My sweet Lucy came up to me – seeing me look so pale and wild – threw her arms round my neck, and leaned forward to kiss me. As she bent her head, I felt the same warm blast rush over my lips, and my sister cried, 'Why, Lizzie, your lips burn like fire!'

And so they did, and for long after. The Presence was with me still, never leaving me day nor night: by my pillow, its whispering voice often waking me from wild dreams; by my side, in the broad sunlight; by my side, in the still moonlight; never absent, busy at my brain, busy at my heart – a form ever banded to me. It flitted like a cold cloud between my sweet sister's eyes and mine, and dimmed them so that I could scarcely see their beauty. It drowned my father's voice; and his words fell confused and indistinct.

Not long after, a stranger came into our neighbourhood. He bought Green Howe, a deserted old property by the riverside, where no one had lived for many many years; not since the young bride, Mrs Braithwaite, had been found in the river one morning, entangled among the dank weeds and dripping alders, strangled and drowned, and her husband dead – none knew how – lying by the chapel door. The place had had a bad name ever since, and no one would live there. However, it was said that a stranger, who had been long in the East, a Mr Felix, had now bought it, and that he was coming to reside there. And, true enough, one day the whole of our little town of Thornhill was in a state of excitement; for a travelling-carriage and four, followed by another full of servants – Hindoos, or Lascars, or Negroes;[7] dark-coloured, strange-looking people – passed through, and Mr Felix took possession of Green Howe.

My father called on him after a time; and I, as the mistress of the house, went with him. Green Howe had been changed, as if by magic, and we both said so together, as we entered the iron gates that led up the broad walk. The ruined garden was one mass of plants, fresh and green, many of them quite new to me; and the shrubbery, which had been a wilderness, was restored to order. The house looked larger than before, now that it was so beautifully decorated; and the broken trellis-work, which used to hang dangling among the ivy, was matted with creeping roses, and jasmine, which left on me the impression of having been in flower, which was impossible. It was a fairy palace; and we could scarcely believe that this was the deserted, ill-omened Green Howe. The foreign servants, too, in Eastern dresses, covered with rings, and necklaces, and earrings; the foreign smells of sandalwood, and camphor, and musk; the curtains that hung everywhere in place of doors, some of velvet, and some of cloth of gold; the air of luxury, such as I, a simple country girl, had never seen before, made such a powerful impression on me, that I felt as if carried away to some unknown region. As we entered, Mr Felix came to meet us; and, drawing aside a heavy curtain that seemed all of gold and fire – for the flame-coloured flowers danced and quivered on the gold – he led us into an inner room, where the darkened light; the atmosphere heavy with perfumes; the statues; the birds like living jewels; the magnificence of stuffs, and the luxuriousness of arrangement, overpowered me. I felt as if I had sunk into a lethargy, in which I heard only the rich voice, and saw only the fine form of our stranger host.

He was certainly very handsome; tall, dark, yet pale as marble: his very lips were pale; with eyes that were extremely bright; but which had an expression behind them that subdued me. His manners were graceful. He was very cordial to us, and made us stay a long time; taking us through his grounds to see his improvements, and pointing out here and there further alterations to be made; all with such a disregard for local difficulties, and for cost, that, had he been one of the princes of the genii[8] he could not have talked more royally. He was more than merely attentive to me; speaking to me often and in a lower voice, bending down near to me, and looking at me with eyes that thrilled through every nerve and fibre. I saw that my father was uneasy; and, when we left, I asked him how he liked our new neighbour. He said, 'Not much, Lizzie,' with a grave and almost displeased look, as if he had probed the weakness I was scarcely conscious of myself. I thought at the time that he was harsh.

However, as there was nothing positively to object to in Mr Felix, my father's impulse of distrust could not well be indulged without rudeness; and my dear father was too thoroughly a gentleman ever to be rude even to his enemy. We therefore saw a great deal of the stranger; who established himself in our house on the most familiar footing, and forced on my father and Lucy an intimacy they both disliked but could not avoid. For it was forced with such consummate skill and tact, that there was nothing which the most rigid could object to.

I gradually became an altered being under his influence. In one thing only a happier – in the loss of the Voice and the Form which had haunted me. Since I had known Felix this terror had gone. The reality had absorbed the shadow. But in nothing else was this strange man's influence over me, beneficial. I remember that I used to hate myself for my excessive irritability of temper when I was away from him. Everything at home displeased me. Everything seemed so small and mean and old and poor after the lordly glory of that house; and the very caresses of my family and olden schoolday friends were irksome and hateful to me. All except my Lucy lost its charm; and to her I was faithful as ever; to her I never changed. But her influence seemed to war with his, wonderfully. When with him I felt borne away in a torrent. His words fell upon me mysterious and thrilling, and he gave me fleeting glimpses into worlds which had never opened themselves to me before; glimpses seen and gone like the Arabian gardens.

When I came back to my sweet sister, her pure eyes and the holy light that lay in them, her gentle voice speaking of the sacred things of heaven and the earnest things of life, seemed to me like a former existence: a state I had lived in years ago. But this divided influence nearly killed me; it seemed to part my very soul and wrench my being in twain; and this, more than all the rest, made me sad beyond anything people believed possible in one so gay and reckless as I had been.

My father's dislike to Felix increased daily; and Lucy, who had never been known to use a harsh word in her life, from the first refused to believe a thought of good in him, or to allow him one single claim to praise. She used to cling to me in a wild, beseeching way, and entreat me with prayers, such as a mother might have poured out before an erring child, to stop in time, and to return to those who loved me. 'For your soul is lost from among us, Lizzie,' she used to say; 'and nothing but a frame remains of the full life of love you once gave us!' But one word, one look, from Felix was enough to make me forget every tear and every prayer of her who, until now, had been my idol and my law.[9]

At last my dear father commanded me not to see Felix again. I felt as if I should have died. In vain I wept and prayed. In vain I gave full licence to my thoughts, and suffered words to pour from my lips which ought never to have crept into my heart. In vain; my father was inexorable.

I was in the drawing room. Suddenly, noiselessly, Felix was beside me. He had not entered by the door which was directly in front of me; and the window was closed. I never could understand this sudden appearance; for I am certain that he had not been concealed.

'Your father has spoken of me, Lizzie?' he said with a singular smile. I was silent.

'And has forbidden you to see me again?' he continued.

'Yes,' I answered, impelled to speak by something stronger than my will.

'And you intend to obey him?'

'No,' I said again, in the same manner, as if I had been talking in a dream.

He smiled again. Who was he so like when he smiled? I could not remember, and yet I knew that he was like someone I had seen – a face that hovered outside my memory, on the horizon, and never floated near enough to be distinctly realised.

'You are right, Lizzie,' he then said; 'there are ties which are stronger than a father's commands – ties which no man has the right, and no man has the power to break. Meet me tomorrow at noon in the Low Lane; we will speak further.'

He did not say this in any supplicating, nor in any loving manner: it was simply a command, unaccompanied by one tender word or look. He had never said he loved me – never; it seemed to be too well understood between us to need assurances.

I answered, 'Yes,' burying my face in my hands, in shame at this my first act of disobedience to my father; and, when I raised my head, he was gone. Gone as he had entered, without a footfall sounding ever so lightly.

I met him the next day; and it was not the only time that I did so. Day after day I stole at his command from the house, to walk with him in the Low Lane – the lane which the country people said was haunted, and which was consequently always deserted. And there we used to walk or sit under the blighted elm tree for hours; – he talking, but I not understanding all he said: for there was a tone of grandeur and of mystery in his words that overpowered without enlightening me, and that left my spirit dazzled rather than convinced. I had to give reasons at home for my long absences, and he bade me say that I had been with old Dame Todd, the blind widow of Thornhill Rise, and that I had been reading the Bible to her. And I obeyed; although, while I said it, I felt Lucy's eyes fixed plaintively on mine, and heard her murmur a prayer that I might be forgiven.

Lucy grew ill. As the flowers and the summer sun came on, her spirit faded more rapidly away. I have known since, that it was grief more than malady which was killing here. The look of nameless suffering, which used to be in her face, has haunted me through life with undying sorrow. It was suffering that I, who ought to have rather died for her, had caused. But not even her illness stayed me. In the intervals I nursed her tenderly and lovingly as before; but for hours and hours I left her – all through the long days of summer – to walk in the Low Lane, and to sit in my world of poetry and fire. When I came back my sister was often weeping, and I knew that it was for me – I, who once would have given my life to save her from one hour of sorrow. Then I would fling myself on my knees beside her, in an agony of shame and repentance, and promise better things of the morrow, and vow strong efforts against the power and the spell that were on me. But the morrow subjected me to the same unhallowed fascination, the same faithlessness.

At last Felix told me that I must come with him; that I must leave my home, and take part in his life; that I belonged to him and to him only, and that I could not break the tablet of a fate ordained; that I was his destiny, and he mine, and that I must fulfil the law which the stars had written in the sky. I fought against this. I spoke of my father's anger, and of my sister's illness. I prayed to him for pity, not to force this on me, and knelt in the shadows of the autumn sunset to ask from him forbearance.

I did not yield this day, nor the next, nor for many days. At last he conquered. When I said 'Yes' he kissed the scarf I wore round my neck. Until then he had never touched even my hand with his lips. I consented to leave my sister, who I well knew was dying; I consented to leave my father, whose whole life had been one act of love and care for his children; and to bring a stain on our name, unstained until then. I consented to leave those who loved me – all I loved – for a stranger.

All was prepared; the hurrying clouds, lead-coloured, and the howling wind, the fit companions in nature with the evil and the despair of my soul. Lucy was worse today; but though I felt going to my death, in leaving her, I could not resist. Had his voice called me to the scaffold, I must have gone. It was the last day of October, and at midnight when I was to leave the house. I had kissed my sleeping sister, who was dreaming in her sleep, and cried, and grasped my hand, and called aloud, 'Lizzie, Lizzie! Come back!' But the spell was on me, and I left her; and still her dreaming voice called out, choking with sobs 'Not there! not there, Lizzie! Come back to me!'

I was to leave the house by the large, old, haunted room that I have spoken of before; Felix waiting for me outside. And, a little after twelve o'clock, I opened the door to pass through. This time the chill, and the damp, and the darkness unnerved me. The broken mirror was in the middle of the room, as before, and, in passing it, I mechanically raised my eyes. Then I remembered that it was Allhallow's Eve, the anniversary of the apparition of last year. As I looked, the room, which had been so deadly still, became filled with the sound I had heard before. The rushing of large wings, and the crowd of whispering voices flowed like a river round me; and again, glaring into my eyes, was the same face in the glass that I had seen before, the sneering smile even more triumphant, the blighting stare of the fiery eyes, the low brow and the coal-black hair, and the look of mockery. All were there; and all I had seen before and since; for it was Felix who was gazing at me from the glass. When I turned to speak to him, the room was empty. Not a living creature was there; only a low laugh, and the far-off voices whispering, and the wings. And then a hand tapped on the window, and the voice of Felix cried from outside, 'Come, Lizzie, come!'

I staggered, rather than walked, to the window; and, as I was close to it – my hand raised to open it – there stood between me and it a pale figure clothed in white; her face more pale than the linen round it. Her hair hung down on her breast, and her blue eyes looked earnestly and mournfully into mine. She was silent, and yet it seemed as if a volume of love and of entreaty flowed from her lips; as if I heard words of deathless affection. It was Lucy; standing there in this bitter midnight cold – giving her life to save me. Felix called to me again, impatiently; and, as he called, the figure turned, and beckoned me; beckoning me gently, lovingly, beseechingly; and then slowly faded away. The chime of the half-hour sounded; and, I fled from the room to my sister. I found her lying dead on the floor; her hair hanging over her breast, and one hand stretched out as if in supplication.

The next day Felix disappeared; he and his whole retinue; and Green Howe fell into ruins again. No one knew where he went, as no one knew from whence he came. And to this day I sometimes doubt whether or not he was a clever adventurer, who had heard of my father's wealth: and who, seeing my weak and imaginative character, had acted on it for his own purposes. All that I do know is that my sister's spirit saved me from ruin; and that she died to save me. She had seen and known all, and gave herself for my salvation down to the last and supreme effort she made to rescue me. She died at that hour of half-past twelve; and at half-past twelve, as I live before you all, she appeared to me and recalled me.

And this is the reason why I never married, and why I pass Allhallow's Eve in prayer by my sister's grave. I have told you tonight this story of mine, because I feel that I shall not live over another last night of October, but that before the next white Christmas roses come out like winter stars on the earth I shall be at peace in the grave. Not in the grave; let me rather hope with my blessed sister in Heaven!

OVER THE WAY'S STORY
[by George A. Sala]

Once upon a time, before I retired from mercantile pursuits
and came to live over the way, I lived, for many years, in
Ursine Lane.

Ursine Lane is a very rich, narrow, dark, dirty, straggling
lane in the great city of London (said by some to be itself
as rich, as dark, and as dirty). Ursine Lane leads from Cheapside into Thames Street, facing Sir John Pigg's wharf; but
whether Ursine Lane be above or below Bow Church, I shall
not tell you. Neither, whether its name be derived from a bear-
garden, (which was in great vogue in its environs in Queen
Bess's time), or from an Ursuline Nunnery which flourished
in its vicinity, before big, bad King Harry sent nuns to spin, or
to do anything else they could.[10] Ursine Lane it was before the
great fire of London, and Ursine Lane it is now.

The houses in Ursine Lane are very old, very inconvenient,
and very dilapidated; and I don't think another great fire
(all the houses being well insured, depend upon it) would do
the neighbourhood any harm, in clearing the rubbishing old
lane away. Number four tumbled in, and across the road on to
number sixteen, a few years ago; and since then, Ursine Lane
has been provided with a species of roofing in the shape
of great wooden beams to shore up its opposite sides. The
district surveyor shakes his head very much at Ursine Lane,
and resides as far from it as he can. The cats of the neighbourhood find great delectation in the shoring beams, using them,
in the night season, as rialtos and bridges, not of sighs, but of
miauws; but foot passengers look wistfully and somewhat
fearfully upwards at these wooden defences. Yet Ursine Lane
remains. To be sure, if you were to pull it down, you would

have to remove the old church of St Nicholas Bearcroft, where the bells ring every Friday night, in conformity with a bequest of Master Miniver Squirrell, furrier, obiit sixteen hundred and eighty-four, piously to commemorate his escape from the paws of a grisly bear while travelling in the wilds of Muscovy. You would have to demolish the brave gilt lion, and the brave gilt unicorn at the extremity of the churchwardens' pew, who (saving their gender) with the clerk, the sexton, and two or three deaf old shopkeepers and their wives, are pretty nearly all the dearly beloved brethren whom the Reverend Tremaine Popples, MA, can gather together as a congregation. Worse than all, if Ursine Lane were to come down, the pump must come down – the old established, constitutional, vested, endowed pump; built, so tradition runs, over a fountain blessed by the great St Ursula herself. So Ursine Lane remains.

At a certain period of the world's history, it may have been yesterday, it may have been yesterday twenty years, there dwelt in this dismal avenue, a Beast. Everybody called him a Beast. He was a Manchester warehouseman. Now it is not at all necessary for a Manchester warehouseman – or, indeed, for any warehouseman – to be a beast or a brute, or anything disagreeable. Quite the contrary. For instance, next door to the Beast's were the counting-houses and warerooms of Tapperly and Grigg, also Manchester warehousemen, as merry, light-hearted, good-humoured young fellows as you would wish to see. Tapperly was somewhat of a sporting character, rode away every afternoon on a high-stepping brown mare, and lounged regularly about the entrance to 'Tats' whether he booked any bets or not. As for Grigg, he was the Coryphaeus of all the middle class *soirées*, dancing academies and subscription balls in London, and it was a moving sight to see him in his famous

Crusader costume at a Drury Lane Bal Masqué.[11] Nor was old Sir William Watch (of the firm of Watch, Watch, and Rover, Manchester warehousemen) at the corner, who was fined so many thousand pounds for smuggling once upon a time, at all beastlike or brutish. He was a white-headed, charitable jolly old gentleman, fond of old port and old songs and old clerks and porters, and his cheque book was as open as his heart. Lacteal, Flewitt, and Company, again, on the other side of the Beast's domicile, the great dealers in gauzes and ribbons, were mild, placable, pious men, the beloved of Clapham. But the Beast was a Beast and no mistake. Everybody said he was; and what everybody says, must be true. His name was Braddlescroggs.

Barnard Braddlescroggs. He was the head, the trunk and the tail of the firm. No Co., no son, no nephew, no brothers: B. BRADDLESCROGGS glared at you from either door jamb. His warerooms were extensive, gloomy, dark, and crowded. So were his counting-houses, which were mostly underground, and candlelit. He loved to keep his subordinates in these dark dens, where he could rush in upon them suddenly, and growl at them. You came wandering through these subterraneans upon wan men, pent up among parasols and *cartons* of gay ribbons; upon pale lads in spectacles registering silks and merinos by the light of flickering, strong-smelling tallow candles in rusty sconces. There was no counting-house community; no desk fellowship: the clerks were isolated – dammed up in steep little pulpits, relegated behind walls of cotton goods, consigned to the *in-pace* of bales of tarlatan and barège.[12] The Beast was everywhere. He prowled about continually. He lurked in holes and corners. He reprimanded clerks on staircases, and discharged porters in dark entries. His deep, harsh, grating voice could ever be heard growling during the hours of business, somewhere, like a sullen earth-quake. His stern Wellington boots continually creaked. His numerous keys rattled gaoler-fashion. His very watch, when wound up, made a savage gnashing noise, as though the works were in torment. He was a Beast.

Tall, square, sinewy, and muscular in person; large and angular in features; with a puissant, rebellious head of grey hair that would have defied all the brushing, combing, and greasing of the Burlington Arcade;[13] with black bushy eyebrows nearly meeting on his forehead; with a horseshoe frown between his eyes; with stubbly whiskers, like horsehair spikes, rather indented in his cheekbones than growing on his cheeks; with a large, stiff, shirt collar and frill defending his face like *chevaux-de-frise;*[14] with large, coarse, bony hands plunged in his trouser pockets; with a great seal and ribbons and the savage ticking watch I have mentioned – such was Barnard Braddlescroggs. From the ears and nostrils of such men you see small hairs growing, indomitable by tweezers; signs of inflexibility of purpose, and stern virility. Their joints crack as they walk. His did.

Very rich, as his father, old Simon Braddlescroggs, had been before him, B. Braddlescroggs was not an avaricious man. He had never been known to lend or advance a penny to the necessitous; but he paid his clerks and servants liberal salaries. This was a little unaccountable in the Beast, but it was said that they did not hate him the less. He gave largely to stern charities, such as dragged sinners to repentance, or administered eleemosynary[15] food, education and blows (in a progressively liberal proportion) to orphan children. He was visiting justice to strict gaols, and was supposed not to have quite made up his mind as to what system of prison discipline was best – unremitting corporal punishment, or continuous solitary confinement. He apprenticed boys to hard trades, or assisted them to emigrate to inclement climates. He was a member of a rigid persuasion, and one high in authority, and had half built a chapel at his own expense; but everybody said that few people thanked him, or were grateful to him for his generosity. He was such a Beast. He bit the orphan's nose off, and bullied the widow. He gave alms as one who pelts a dog with marrow-bones, hurting him while he feeds him. Those in his employment who embezzled or robbed him, were it of but a penny piece, he mercilessly prosecuted to conviction. Everybody had observed it. He sued all debtors, opposed all insolvents, and strove to bring all bankrupts within the meaning of the penal clauses. Everybody knew it. The merchants and brokers, his compeers, fell away from him on 'Change;[16] his correspondents opened his hard, fierce letters with palpitating hearts; his clerks cowered before him; his maid servants passed him (when they had courage to pass him at all) with fear and trembling. The waiters at the Cock in Threadneedle Street, where he took a fiery bowl of Mulligatawny soup[17] for lunch, daily, didn't like him. At his club at the West End he had a bow window and a pile of newspapers all to himself – dined by himself – drank by himself – growled to himself.

There had been a Mrs Braddlescroggs; a delicate, blue-eyed little woman out of Devonshire, who had been Beauty to the Beast. She died early. Her husband was not reported to have beaten her, or starved her, or verbally ill-treated her, but simply to have frightened her to death. Everybody said so. She could never take those mild blue eyes of hers off her terrible husband, and died – looking at him timorously. One son had been born to B.B. at her demise. He grew up a pale, fair-haired, frightened lad, with his mother's eyes. The Beast had treated him (everybody was indignant at it) from his earliest years with unvarying and consistent severity; and at fourteen he was removed from the school of the rigid persuasion, where he had received his dreary commercial education, to his father's rigider, drearier establishment in Ursine Lane. He had a department to himself there, and a tallow candle to himself.

The clerks, some twelve in number, all dined and slept in the house. They had a dismal dormitory over some stables in Grizzly Buildings, at the back of Ursine Lane; and dined in a dingy, uncarpeted room at the top of the building – on one unvarying bill of fare of beef, mutton, and potatoes – plenty of it, though, for the Beast never stinted them: which was remarkable in *such* a Beast. The domestic arrangements were superintended by a housekeeper – a tall, melancholy, middle-aged lady, supposed to have been once in affluent circumstances. She had been very good-looking, too, once, but had something the matter with her spine, and not unfrequently fell downstairs, or upstairs, in fits of syncope.[18] When the Beast had no one else to abuse and maltreat, he would go upstairs and abuse Mrs Plimmets, and threaten her with dismissal and inevitable starvation. Business hours concluded at eight nightly, and from that hour to ten P.M. the clerks were permitted to walk where they listed – but exclusion and expulsion were the never failing result of a moment's unpunctuality in returning home. The porters slept out of the house, and the clerks looked at them almost as superior beings – as men of strange experiences and knowledge of life – men who had been present at orgies prolonged beyond midnight – men who had remained in the galleries of theatres till the performances were concluded.

Of the dozen clerks who kept the books of Barnard Braddlescroggs (save that grim auriferous[19] banker's passbook of his) and registered his wares, I have to deal with but two. My business lies only with blue-eyed, pale-faced William Braddlescroggs, and with John Simcox the corresponding clerk.

Simcox among his fellow clerks, Mr Simcox among the porters, Jack Simcox among his intimates at the Admiral Benbow near Camberwell Gate, 'you Simcox', with his growling chief. A grey-haired, smiling, red-faced simpleton was Simcox; kind of heart, simple of mind, affectionate of disposition, confiding of nature, infirm of purpose, convivial of habits. He was fifty years in age, and fifteen in wisdom. He had been at the top of the ladder once – a rich man at least by paternal inheritance, with a carriage and horses and lands; but when he tumbled (which he did at five-and-twenty, very quickly and right to the bottom), he never managed to rise again. The dupe of every shallow knave; the victim in every egregious scheme; an excellent arithmetician, yet quite unable to put two and two together in a business sense; he had never even had strength of character to be his own enemy; he had always found such a multiplicity of friends ready to do the inimical for him. If you let him alone he would do well enough. He would not lose his money till you cheated him out of it; he would not get drunk himself, but would allow you to make him so, with the most charming willingness and equanimity. There are many Simcoxes in the world, and more rogues always ready to prey upon them; yet though I should like to hang the rogues, I should not like to see the breed of Simcox quite extinct.

John Simcox had a salary of one hundred and twenty pounds a year. If I were writing fiction instead of sober (though veiled) truth, I should picture him to you as a victim with some two score of sovereigns per annum. No; he had a hundred and twenty of those yellow tokens annually – for the Beast never stinted in this respect either: which was again remarkable in such a Beast. One hundred and twenty golden sovereigns annually, had John Simcox; and they were of about as much use to him as one hundred and twenty penny pieces. When a man has a quarter's salary amounting to twenty-seven pounds, receivable next Thursday, and out of that has a score of three pounds due at the Admiral Benbow, and has promised to (and will) lend ten pounds to a friend, and has borrowed five more of another friend himself, which he means to pay; and has besides his little rent to meet, and his little butcher and his little grocer and his little tailor, it is not very difficult to imagine how the man may be considerably embarrassed in satisfying all these demands out of the capital. But, when the administrator of the capital happens to be (as Simcox was) a man without the slightest command of himself or his money – you will have no difficulty in forming a conviction that the end of Simcox's quarter days were worse than their commencement.

Nor will you be surprised that 'executions' in Simcox's little house in Carolina Terrace, Albany Road, Camberwell, were of frequent occurrence; that writs against him were always 'out', and the brokers always 'in'. That he was as well known in the county court as the judge. That orders for payment were always coming due and never being paid. His creditors never arrested him, however. If they did so, they knew he would lose his situation; so the poor man went on from week to week, and from month to month, borrowing here and borrowing there, obtaining small advances from loan societies held at public houses,[20] robbing Peter to pay Paul – always in a muddle, in short; but still smoking his nightly pipes, and drinking his nightly glasses, and singing his nightly songs; the latter with immense applause at the Admiral Benbow.

I don't think Simcox's worldly position was at all improved by his having married (in very early life, and direct from the finishing establishment of the Misses Gimp, at Hammersmith) a young lady highly accomplished in the useful and productive arts of tambour-work and Poonah painting; but of all domestic or household duties considerably more ignorant than a Zooloo Kaffir.[21] When Simcox had run through his money, an operation he performed with astonishing celerity, Mrs Simcox, finding herself with three daughters of tender age and a ruined husband, took refuge in floods of tears; subsequently met the crisis of misfortune with a nervous fever; and ultimately subsided into permanent ill health, curl papers, and shoes down at heel.

When the events took places herein narrated, the three daughters of Mr and Mrs Simcox were all grown up. Madeline, aged twenty-two, was a young lady of surprising altitude, with shoulders of great breadth and sharpness of outline, with very large black eyes and very large black ringlets, attributes of which she was consciously proud, but with a nose approaching to – what shall I say? – the snub. Chemists' assistants had addressed acrostics[22] to her; and the young man at the circulating library was supposed to be madly in love with her. Helena, daughter number two, aged twenty, was also tall, had also black eyes, black ringlets, white resplendent shoulders, was the beloved of apothecaries, and the Laura of Petrarchs[23] in the linen-drapery line. These young ladies were both acknowledged, recognised, established as beauties in the Camberwellian district. They dressed, somehow, in the brightest and most variegated colours; they had, somehow, the prettiest of bonnets, the tightest of gloves, the neatest of kid boots. Their sabbatical entrance to the parish church always created a sensation. The chemist's assistant kissed his hand as they passed; the young man at the circulating library laid down his book, and sighed; passing young ladies envied and disparaged; passing young gentlemen admired and aspired; yet, somehow, Miss Madeline would be twenty-three next birthday, and Miss Helena twenty-one, and no swain had yet declared himself in explicit terms; no one had said, 'I have a hundred a year, with a prospect of an advance: take it, my heart, and hand.' Old Muggers, indeed, the tailor of Acacia Cottages, the friend, creditor, and boon companion of Simcox, had intimated, in his cups, at the Admiral Benbow, his willingness to marry either of the young ladies; but his matrimonial proposals generally vanished with his inebriety; and he was besides known to be a dreadfully wicked old man, addicted to drinking, smoking, and snuff-taking. As a climax of villany, he was supposed to have two wives already, alive, and resident in different parts of the provinces.

And daughter number three – have I forgotten her? Not by any means. Was she a beauty? No. In the opinion of her sisters, of Camberwell, and of the chemist's assistant, she was *not* a beauty. She had dark eyes; but they were neither brilliant nor piercing. She had dark hair; but wore it in no long or resplendent ringlets. She was an ordinary girl, a 'plain little thing' (according to the Camberwell opinion); there was 'nothing about her' in the eyes of the chemist's assistant.

This young person (Bessy by name), from the earliest periods of authentic record to the mature age of sixteen, had occupied, in the Simcox household, an analogous position to that of the celebrated Cinderella. She did not exactly sit in the chimney corner among the ashes; but she lighted the fire, waited upon, dressed, and was otherwise the humble and willing drudge of her accomplished relatives. She did not exactly dress in rags; but she trotted about the house and neighbourhood in a shabby brown merino frock, which she had wofully outgrown, a lamentable old beaver bonnet, and a faded Paisley shawl which held a sort of middle rank in appearance, between a duster and a pocket handkerchief well to do in the world. As a child, she was punished for the things she did not do, and doubly punished for those she did do. As a girl, she ran of errands, fetched the beer, lighted the fire (as I have said), read the sentimental novels to her mamma as she lay upon the sofa, and accompanied her sisters on the pianoforte when they rehearsed those famous songs and duets with which they did terrific execution in the Camberwell circles.

Honest Simcox, like a stupid, undiscerning shiftless man as he was, did not entertain the domestic or Camberwell opinion concerning Bessy. He maintained that she had more sense in her little finger than her sisters put together (with his wife into the bargain, the honest fellow thought, I dare swear, though he did not dare to say so). He called her his little darling, his little Mentor, his willing, patient Betsy-petsy, with other foolish and weak-minded expressions of endearment. What else could you expect of a red-nosed warehouseman's clerk who fuddled himself nightly at the Admiral Benbow! Profoundly submissive to his wife in most instances, he had frequently presumed, during Bessy's nonage,[24] to differ from Mrs Simcox as to the amount of whipping meted out to his youngest daughter for childish delinquencies, and had once even dared to interfere when his lady undertook to inflict that punishment for a fault the child had never committed, and to 'stay justice in its mid career'. So in process of time the alliance between the snubbed, neglected little girl and her father became of so close a nature as to be almost recognised and permitted by the rest of the family. Bessy was reckoned among the rest of the low company with whom the degraded

Simcox chose to associate. She was allowed to pull off his muddy boots, to prepare his dinner, to fill his pipe and mix his grog when he muddled himself at home; and to lead him home, shambling, from the Admiral Benbow, when he performed that operation abroad.

Notably of late times she had been commissioned to fetch her papa home from Ursine Lane on the eventful quarter day; and the meek guiding help of Bessy had often saved that infirm old fellow from many a dark and dangerous pitfall. The child would wait patiently outside the doors of public houses while her father boozed within; she would lead him away gently but firmly from his riotous companions, or, meeting them and taking them aside, would plead passionately, tearfully, that they would not make papa tipsy tonight. Some of the disreputable personages with whom she was brought into such strange contact were quite subdued and abashed by her earnest, artless looks and speech. Jack Flooks himself, formerly of the Stock Exchange, now principally of the bar of the Bag o' Nails, the very worst, most dissipated and most reckless of Simcox's associates forbore drinking with Bessy's father for one whole week, and actually returned, in a private and mysterious manner, to Bessy two half-crowns he had borrowed of him! So useful was this filial surveillance found to be by the other branches of his family that the quarter-day functions of our plain little Bessy were gradually extended, and became next of weekly and afterwards of diurnal occurrence.

It was good to see this girl arrayed in the forlorn beaver bonnet and the faded Paisley shawl, with her mild, beaming, ordinary, little countenance, arrive at about a quarter to eight at the Thames Street corner of Ursine Lane, and there wait patiently until her father's official duties were over. She became almost as well known in the neighbourhood as St

Nicholas Bearward, or as the famous sanctified pump itself. The fellowship porters from Sir John Pigg's wharf touched their caps to her; the majestic beadle of St Nicholas (a cunning man, omnipotent over the fire escape, king of the keys of the engine-house, and supposed to know where the fireplug was, much better than the turncock) spoke her kindly; all the clerks in Braddlescroggs's house knew her, nodded to her, smiled at her, and privately expressed their mutual opinions as to what a beast Braddlescroggs was, not to ask that dear little girl in, and let her rest herself, or sit by the fire in winter. The potboy of the Bear and Ragged Staff, in his evening excursions with the supper beer, grew quite enamoured (in his silent, sheepish fashion) of this affectionate daughter, and would, I dare say, had he dared, have offered her refreshment from his beer can; nay, even the majestic wealthy Mr Drum, the wholesale grocer and provision merchant, who stood all day with his hands in his pockets, under his own gibbet-like crane, a very Jack Ketch of West India produce,[25] had addressed cheering and benevolent words to her from the depths of his double chin; had conferred figs upon her; had pressed her to enter his saccharine-smelling warehouse, and rest herself upon a barrel of prime navy mess beef.

When the Beast of Ursine Lane met Bessy Simcox he either scowled at her, or made her sarcastic bows, and asked her at what pot-house[26] her father was about to get drunk that night, and whether he had taught *her* to drink gin, too? Sometimes he growled forth his determination to have no 'bits of girls' hanging about his 'place'; sometimes he told her that she would not have to come many times more, for that he was determined on discharging that 'drunken old dog', her papa. In the majority of instances, however, he passed her without any other notice than a scowl, and a savage rattle of the keys and silver in his pockets. The little maiden trembled fearfully when she saw him, and had quiet fits of weeping (in which a corner of the Paisley shawl was brought into frequent requisition) over against the pump, when he had spoken to her. There was a lad called William Braddlescroggs, with blue eyes and fair hair, who blushed very violently whenever he saw Bessy, and had once been bold enough to tell her that it was a fine evening. In this flagrant crime he was then and there detected by his father, who drove him back into the warehouse.

'As this is quarter day, my Bessy,' was the remark of John Simcox to his daughter, one twenty-eighth of March, 'as this is quarter day, I think, my child, that I will take one glass of ale.'

It was about half-past eight, I think, and Bessy and her papa were traversing the large thoroughfare known as the New Kent Road. There is in that vicinity, as you are aware, that stunning Champagne Ale House, known as the Leather Bottel. Into that stunning ale house did John Simcox enter, leaving his little Bessy outside, with fifteen pounds, the balance of what he had already expended of his quarter's salary. The night was very lowering, and rain appeared to be imminent. It came down, presently, in big, pattering drops, but John had promised not to be long.

Why should I tell, *in extenso*, the humiliating tale of how John Simcox got tipsy that night? How he forced all the money, pound by pound, from his little daughter? How, when after immense labour and trouble, he had at last been brought to his own street door, he suddenly started off at an unknown tangent (running hard and straight), and disappeared. How his daughter wandered about, weeping, in the pouring rain, seeking him; how, at two o'clock in the morning, a doleful party arrived at a little house in Camberwell – a very moist policeman, a weeping, shivering, drenched little girl over whom the municipal had in pity thrown his oilskin cape, and a penniless, hatless, drunken man, all covered with mud, utterly sodden, wretched, and degraded. Drop the curtain for pity's sake.

The first impulse of Mrs Simcox, after duly loading her besotted husband with reproaches, was to beat Bessy. The anger of this matron, generally so gently languid, was something fearful to view. An enraged sheep is frantic. She was frustrated, however, in her benevolent intention, first by the policeman, afterwards by Bessy herself, who, wet, fatigued, and miserable (but in an artful and designing manner, no doubt), first contrived to faint away, and next day chose to fall into a high fever.

In this fever – in the access therefore – she lay three long weeks. In a lamentable state of languor, she lay many long weeks more. The brokers were in again. The parlour carpet was taken up and sent to the pawnbroker's. There were no invalid comforts in the house; no broth, nor chickens to make it, no arrowroot, no sago,[27] no Port wine, no anything to speak of, that was really wanted.

Stay, I am wrong. There were plenty of doctors; there was plenty of doctor's stuff. The chemists, apothecaries, and medical practitioners of the neighbourhood, treated the Simcox family, and the little sick daughter, in particular, in a liberal and considerate manner. Not one charged a penny, and all were unremitting in attention. Kind-hearted Mr Sphoon, of Walworth, sent in – so to speak – a hamper of quinine. Young Tuckett, close by, who had just passed the Hall and College, and opened his shop, offered to do anything for Bessy. He would have dissected her even, I am sure. Great Doctor Bibby came from Camberwell Grove, in his own carriage, with his own footman with the black worsted tags on his shoulder, and majestically ordered change of air, and red Port wine for

Bessy Simcox. A majestic man was Dr Bibby, and a portly, and a deep-voiced, and a rich. His boots creaked, and his carriage springs oscillated – but he left a sovereign on the Simcox mantelpiece, for all that.

So there was something of those things needful in the little house at Camberwell. There was besides, a certain nurse, active, devoted, patient, soothing, and gentle. Not Mrs Simcox, who still lay on the sofa, now reading the sentimental novels, now moaning over the family difficulties. Not the Misses Simcox, who though they did tend their sister, did it very fretfully and cross-grainedly, and unanimously declared that the child made herself out to be a great deal worse than she really was. This nurse had rather a red nose, and a tremulous hand. He came home earlier from the City now; but he never stopped at the stunning Champagne Ale House. He had not been to the Admiral Benbow for seven weeks. He sat by his daughter's pillow; he read to her; he carried her in his arms like a child as she was; he wept over the injury he had done her; he promised, and meant, and prayed for, amendment.

But what were the attentions of the doctors, the hamper of quinine, the sovereign on the mantelpiece, even, after all? They were but drops in the great muddled ocean of the Simcox embarrassments. A sovereign would not take Bessy to Malvern or Ventnor;[28] the quinine would not give her red Port wine and change of air. The nurse grew desperate. There was no money to be borrowed, none to be obtained from the pawnbroker, none to be received until next quarter day – before which, another month must elapse. Should he attempt to obtain a small advance of money from the Beast himself – the terrible Braddlescroggs? Should he offer him two hundred per cent. interest; should he fall down on his knees before him; should he write him a supplicatory letter; should he?

One evening, Simcox came home from the office with many smiles upon his face. He had borrowed the money, after many difficulties, from the chief clerk. Ten pounds. He would have to pay very heavy interest for it, but never mind. Mrs Simcox should take Bessy to Ventnor for a fortnight or three weeks. Quarter day would soon come round. Soon come round. Now and then his family remarked, that the many smiles dropped from their papa's countenance like a mask, and that, underneath, he wore a look rather haggard, rather weary, rather terrible; but then, you see, he would have to pay such a heavy interest for the ten pounds. Mrs Simcox was delighted at the prospect of her country trip; poor Bessy smiled and thanked her papa; and the two Miss Simcoxes – who had their own private conviction that an excursion to the seaside was the very thing for them; to air their beauty as it were – and not for that designing bit of a thing, Bessy, with her pale face – the two Miss Simcoxes, I say, went to bed in a huff.

To the pleasant Island of Wight in the British Channel, and the country of Hampshire did the little convalescent from Camberwell and her parent proceed. Bessy gathered shells and seaweeds, and bought sand pictures on cardboard by the Undercliff, and sand in bottles, and saw the donkey at Carisbroke Castle, and wondered at Little St Lawrence Church, and the magnificent yachting dandies at Cowes and Ryde, until her pale face grew quite rosy, and her dark eyes had something of a sparkle in them. Her mamma lay on the sofa as usual, exhausted the stock of sentimental novels in the Ventnor circulating library, varying these home occupations occasionally by taking exercise in a wheelchair, and 'nagging' at Bessy. The pair came back to London together, and were at the little mansion at Camberwell about a week before quarter day. The peccant Simcox had been exemplarily abstemious during their absence; but his daughters had not been able to avoid remarking that he was silent, reserved, and anxious looking. You see he had to pay such heavy interest for the ten pounds he had borrowed of the chief clerk.

Three days before quarter day, it was ten minutes to eight P.M., and Bessy Simcox was waiting for her father. She was confident, hopeful, cheerful now: she thanked God for her illness and the change it had wrought in her dear papa. Ten minutes to eight, and a hot summer's evening. She was watching the lamplighter going round with his ladder and his little glimmering lantern, when she was accosted by one of Mr Braddlescroggs's porters. He was an ugly forbidding man with a vicious-looking fur cap (such as porters of workhouses and wicked skippers of colliers wear), and had never before saluted or spoken to her. She began to tremble violently when John Malingerer (a special favourite of the Beast's, if he could have favoured any one, and supposed to be a porter after his own heart), addressed her.

'Hi!' said the porter, 'you're wanted.'

'Me – wanted? Where? By whom?' stammered Bessy.

'Counting-house – Governor – Bisness,' replied John Malingerer, in short growling periods.

Bessy followed him, still trembling. The porter walked before her, looming like the genius of Misfortune. He led her through dingy wareroom after wareroom, counting-house after counting-house, where the clerks all were silent and subdued. He led her at last into a dingy sanctum, dimly lighted by one shaded lamp. In this safe there were piles of dingy papers and more dingy ledgers; great piles of accounts on hooks in the wall, with their long iron necks and white bodies like ghosts of dead bills who had hanged themselves; a huge iron safe throwing hideous shadows against the wall, and three silent men.

That is to say:

John Simcox, white, trembling and with wild eyes.

The Beast, neither more nor less a Beast than he usually was.

A tall man with a very sharp shirt collar, a great coat, a black stock; very thin iron-grey hair; a face which looked as if it had once been full of wrinkles and furrows which had been half ironed out; very peculiar and very heavy boots, brown berlin gloves, and a demeanour which confirmed you immediately in a conviction that were you to strike at him violently with a sledge hammer, his frame would give forth in response no fleshy 'thud', but a hard metallic ring.

The Beast was standing up: his back against a tall desk on spectral legs, his hands in his pockets. So also, standing, in a corner, was Simcox. So also, not exactly anywhere but somewhere, somehow, and about Simcox, and about Bessy, and particularly about the door and the iron-safe, in which he seemed to take absorbing interest, was the tall man in the peculiar boots.

'Come here, my girl,' said the grating voice of Barnard Braddlescroggs the Beast.

My girl came there, to the foot of a table, as she was desired. She heard the grating voice; she heard, much louder, the beating of her own heart; she heard, loudest of all, a dreadful voice within her crying over and over again that papa had borrowed ten pounds, and that he would have to pay very heavy interest for it, and that quarter day would soon come round, soon come round.

'This person's name is Lurcher,' pursued the Beast.

The person coughed. The cough struck on the girl's heart like a knell. One.

'He is an officer.'

An officer of what? Of the Household Brigade; of the yeomanry cavalry; of the Sheriff of Middlesex's batallion, a custom-house officer, a naval officer, a relieving officer? But Bessy knew in a moment. She might have known it at first from the peculiar boots the officer wore – boots such as no other officer, or man, or woman can wear. But her own heart told her. It said plainly: 'This is a police officer, and he has come to take your father into custody.'

It was all told directly. Oh Bessy, Bessy! The ten pounds borrowed from the chief clerk, for which he would have to pay such heavy interest. The ten pounds were borrowed from the Petty Cash. The miserable Simcox's account was fifteen pounds deficient; he had promised to refund the money on quarter day; he had begged and prayed for time; the Beast was inexorable, and Lurcher, the officer, was there to take him to prison for embezzlement.

'You daughter of this man,' said the Beast; 'you must go home without him. You tell his wife, and the rest of his people, that I have locked him up, and that I'll transport him, for robbery.'

'Robbery, no, sir,' cried poor Simcox from the corner. 'Before God, no! It was only for – '

'Silence!' said the Beast. 'I'll prosecute you, I'll transport you, I'll hang you. By G—, I'll reform you, somehow. Girl,' he continued, turning to Bessy. 'Go home. Stop! I'll send a clerk with you to see if there are any of my goods at home. I dare say there are, and you'll move 'em tonight. You won't though. I'll have a search warrant. I'll put you all in gaol. I'll transport you all. Come here, one of you fellows in the office' (this with a roar), 'and go with this girl to Camberwell. Lurcher, take the rascal away.'

What was poor Bessy to do? What could she do but fall down on her knees, clasping those stern knees before her?

What could she do, but amid sobs and broken articulation say that it was all her fault? That it was for her, her dear papa had taken the money. That for her use it had been spent. What could she do but implore the Beast, for the love of heaven, for the love of his own son, for the love of his dead father and mother, to spare the object of his wrath, to send her to prison, to take all they had, to show them mercy, as he hoped mercy to be shown to him hereafter?

She did all this and more. It was good, though pitiful, to see the child on her knees in her mean dress, with her streaming eyes, and her poor hair all hanging about her eyes, and to hear her artless, yet passionate supplications. The Beast moved nor muscle nor face; but it is upon record that Mr Lurcher, after creaking about on the peculiar boots for some seconds, turned aside into the shadow of the iron safe, and blew his nose.

'Lurcher,' observed the Beast, 'Wait a moment before I give this man into your charge.'

Mr Lurcher bent some portion of his body between his occiput[29] and his spine, and, considering himself temporarily relieved from the custody of his prisoner, threw the whole force of his contemplative energies into the iron safe, in which, as a subject, he appeared immediately to bury himself.

'Come here!' was the monosyllabic command of the Beast; addressed both to father and daughter. He led them into yet an inner sanctum, a sort of cupboard, full of books and papers, where there was a dreadful screw copying press, like an instrument of torture in the Inquisition.

'I will spare your father, child, and retain him in his situation,' continued the Beast, without ever taking his hands from his pockets, or altering an inflection of his voice, 'on these, and these conditions only. My housekeeper is old and blind, and I shall soon turn her adrift, and let her go to the workhouse – everybody says so, I believe. The short time she will remain, she will be able to instruct you in as much as I shall require of you. You will have to keep this house for me and my clerks, and you must never quit it save once in six weeks, for six hours at a time; and I expect you to adhere to this engagement for two years. All communication between you and your family, save during your hours of liberty, I strictly prohibit. You will have twenty pounds a year as wages, half of which can go to augment your father's salary. At the same time I shall require from him a written acknowledgement that he has embezzled my monies; and if you quit my service I shall use it against him, ruin him, and imprison him. Make up your mind quickly, for the policeman is waiting.'

What was poor Bessy to do? To part from her dear father, never to see him save at intervals, and then only for a short time; to know that he was in the same house, and not be able to run and embrace him! All this was hard, very hard, but what would not Bessy do to save her father from ruin and disgrace and a prison? She would have laid down her life for him, she would have cheerfully consented never to see him again – till the great day comes, when we shall all meet to part no more. She consented. Mr Lurcher was privately spoken to and dismissed; the Beast subsided into his usual taciturnity; Bessy led her stricken, broken, trembling parent home. They passed through the long dingy warerooms: the clerks whispering and looking as they passed.

Bessy's wardrobe was not sufficiently voluminous to occasion the expenditure of any very great time in packing. It was soon put up, in a very small, shabby black box, studded with brass nails – many of them deficient. This, with Bessy herself, arrived at nine o'clock the next morning, as per agreement, at the Cheapside corner of Ursine Lane, where one of

Mr Braddlescroggs's porters was in waiting; who brought Bessy and her box to the dismal Manchester warehouse owned by the Beast of Ursine Lane.

And here, in the top floor of this lugubrious mansion, lived, for two long years, Bessy Simcox. At stated periods she saw her family for a few hours, and then went back to her prison-house. She carved the beef and mutton for the hungry clerks, she mended their linen, she gave out candles, she calculated washing bills. The old, old story of Beauty and the Beast was being done over again in Ursine Lane, Cheapside. Bessy ripened into a Beauty, in this dismal hothouse; and the Beast was – as I have told you he always was. Beauty dwelt in no fairy palace; surrounded by no rosebushes, no sweet-smelling gardens, no invisible hands to wait on her at supper. It was all hard, stern, uncompromising reality. She had to deal with an imperious, sullen, brutal master. Everybody knew it. She dealt with him as Bessy had the art of dealing with everyone. She bore with him meekly, gently, patiently. She strove to win his forbearance, his respect. She won them both, and more – his love.

Yes, his love! Don't be afraid: the Beast never changed to Prince Azor.[30] He never lay among the rosebushes sick to death, and threatening to die unless Beauty married him. But at the end of the two years – when their contract was at an end, and when its fulfilment had given him time to know Bessy well, and to save the father through the child – he besought Bessy to remain with him in the same capacity, offering her munificent terms and any degree of liberty she required as regarded communication with her family. Bessy stayed. She stayed two years; she stayed three; she stays there, now, to witness if I lie.

Not alone however. It occurred to William B., junior – the lad with the blue eyes and fair hair – to grow up to be a tall young man, and to fall violently in love with the pretty little housekeeper. It occurred to his father, instead of smiting him on the hip immediately, or eating him up alive in wild beast fashion,[31] to tell him he was a very sensible fellow, and to incite Bessy (we must call her Beauty now) to encourage his addresses, which indeed, dear little puss! she was nothing loth to do. So Beauty was married. Not to the Beast, but to the Beast's son; and Beauty and William and the Beast all removed to a pretty house in the prettiest country near London, where they dwell to this day, again to witness if I lie.

The Beast is a Beast no longer. Everybody admits that he is not a Beast now; some few are even doubtful whether he ever *was* a Beast. He carries on the Ursine Lane business (in partnership with his son) still, and is a very rough-headed and rough-voiced old man. But the rough kernel and rough integument[32] are worn away from his heart, and he is genial and jovial among his dependents. Charitable in secret, he had always been, even in his most brutish times; and you are not to believe (for Braddlescroggs talked nonsense sometimes and he knew it) that the old housekeeper, when she became blind or bedridden was sent adrift or to the workhouse; that old John Simcox was not allowed sufficient funds for his pipe and his glass (in strict moderation) at the Admiral Benbow; or that the two Misses Simcox, when they married at last (after superhuman exertions), went dowerless. No. The Beast remembered, and was generous to them all.

THE ANGEL'S STORY
[by Adelaide Anne Procter]

Through the blue and frosty heavens,
    Christmas stars were shining bright;
The glistening lamps of the great City
    Almost matched their gleaming light;
And the winter snow was lying,
And the winter winds were sighing,
    Long ago one Christmas night.

While from every tower and steeple,
    Pealing bells were sounding clear,
(Never with such tones of gladness,
    Save when Christmas time is near)
Many a one that night was merry
    Who had toiled through all the year.

That night saw old wrongs forgiven,
    Friends, long parted, reconcile;
Voices, all unused to laughter,
    Eyes that had forgot to smile,
Anxious hearts that feared the morrow,
    Freed from all their care awhile.

Rich and poor felt the same blessing
    From the gracious season fall;
Joy and plenty in the cottage;
    Peace and Feasting in the hall;
And the voices of the children
    Ringing clear above it all!

Yet one house was dim and darkened:
    Gloom, and sickness, and despair
Abiding in the gilded chamber,
    Climbing up the marble stair,
Stilling even the voice of mourning –
    For a child lay dying there.

Silken curtains fell around him,
    Velvet carpets hushed the tread,
Many costly toys were lying,
    All unheeded, by his bed;
And his tangled golden ringlets
    Were on downy pillows spread.

All the skill of the great City
    To save that little life was vain;
That little thread from being broken;
That fatal word from being spoken;
    Nay, his very mother's pain,
And the mighty love within her,
    Could not give him health again.

And she knelt there still beside him,
    She alone with strength to smile,
And to promise he should suffer
    No more in a little while,
And with murmur'd song and story
    The long weary hours beguile.

Suddenly an unseen Presence
    Checked those constant moaning cries,
Stilled the little heart's quick fluttering,

Raised the blue and wondering eyes,
Fixed on some mysterious vision,
    With a startled sweet surprise.

For a radiant angel hovered
    Smiling o'er the little bed;
White his raiment, from his shoulders
    Snowy dove-like pinions spread,
And a starlike light was shining
    In a Glory round his head.

While, with tender love, the angel
    Leaning o'er the little nest,
In his arms the sick child folding,
    Laid him gently on his breast.
Sobs and wailings from the mother,
    And her darling was at rest.

So the angel, slowly rising,
    Spread his wings; and, through the air,
Bore the pretty child, and held him
    On his heart with loving care,
A red branch of blooming roses
    Placing softly by him there.

While the child thus clinging, floated
    Towards the mansions of the Blest,
Gazing from his shining guardian
    To the flowers upon his breast,
Thus the angel spake, still smiling
    On the little heavenly guest:

'Know, O little one! that Heaven
  Does no earthly thing disdain,
Man's poor joys find there an echo
  Just as surely as his pain;
Love, on earth so feebly striving,
  Lives divine in Heaven again!

'Once, in yonder town below us,
  In a poor and narrow street,
Dwelt a little sickly orphan.
  Gentle aid, or pity sweet,
Never in life's rugged pathway
  Guided his poor tottering feet.

'All the striving anxious forethought
  That should only come with age,
Weighed upon his baby spirit,
  Showed him soon life's sternest page;
Grim Want was his nurse, and Sorrow
  Was his only heritage!

'All too weak for childish pastimes
  Drearily the hours sped;
On his hands so small and trembling
  Leaning his poor arching head,
Or, through dark and painful hours,
  Lying sleepless on no bed.

'Dreaming strange and longing fancies
  Of cool forests far away;
Dreams of rosy happy children,
  Laughing merrily at play;

Coming home through green lanes, bearing
  Trailing branches of white May.[33]

'Scarce a glimpse of the blue heavens
  Gleamed above the narrow street,
And the sultry air of Summer
  (That you called so warm and sweet,)
Fevered the poor Orphan, dwelling
  In the crowded alley's heat.

'One bright day, with feeble footsteps
  Slowly forth he dared to crawl,
Through the crowded city's pathways,
  Till he reached a garden wall;
Where 'mid princely halls and mansions
  Stood the lordliest of all.

'There were trees with giant branches,
  Velvet glades where shadows hide;
There were sparkling fountains glancing,
  Flowers whose rich luxuriant pride
Wafted a breath of precious perfume
  To the child who stood outside.

'He against the gate of iron
  Pressed his wan and wistful face,
Gazing with an awestruck pleasure
  At the glories of the place;
Never had his fairest daydream
  Shone with half such wondrous grace.

'You were playing in that garden,
    Throwing blossoms in the air,
And laughing when the petals floated
    Downward on your golden hair;
And the fond eyes watching o'er you,
And the splendour spread before you,
    Told, a House's Hope was there.

'When your servants, tired of seeing
    His pale face of want and woe,
Turning to the ragged Orphan,
    Gave him coin, and bade him go,
Down his cheeks so thin and wasted,
    Bitter tears began to flow.

'But that look of childish sorrow
    On your tender young heart fell,
And you plucked the reddest roses
    From the tree you loved so well,
Passing them through the stern grating,
    With the gentle word, "Farewell!"

'Dazzled by the fragrant treasure
    And the gentle voice he heard,
In the poor forlorn boy's spirit,
    Joy the sleeping Seraph[34] stirred;
In his hand he clasped the flowers,
    In his heart the loving word.

'So he crept to his poor garret,
    Poor no more, but rich and bright;
For the holy dreams of childhood –

Love, and Rest, and Hope, and Light –
Floated round the Orphan's pillow
    Through the starry summer night.

'Day dawned, yet the visions lasted;
    All too weak to rise he lay;
Did he dream that none spake harshly –
    All were strangely kind that day?
Yes; he thought his treasured roses
    Must have charmed all ills away.

'And he smiled, though they were fading;
    One by one their leaves were shed;
"Such bright things could never perish,
    They would bloom again," he said.
When the next day's sun had risen
    Child and flowers both were dead.

'Know, dear little one! our Father
    Does no gentle deed disdain;
And in hearts that beat in heaven,
    Still all tender thoughts remain;
Love on the cold earth beginning
    Lives divine and pure again!'

Thus the angel ceased, and gently
    O'er his little burthen leant;
While the child gazed from the shining
    Loving eyes that o'er him bent,
To the blooming roses by him,
    Wondering what that mystery meant.

Then the radiant angel answered,
    And with holy meaning smiled:
'Ere your tender, loving spirit
    Sin and the hard world defiled,
Mercy gave me leave to seek you; –
    I was once that little child!'

THE SQUIRE'S STORY
[by Elizabeth Gaskell]

In the year seventeen hundred and sixty-nine, the little town of Barford was thrown into a state of great excitement by the intelligence that a gentleman (and 'quite the gentleman,' said the landlord of the George Inn), had been looking at Mr Clavering's old house. This house was neither in the town nor in the country. It stood on the outskirts of Barford, on the roadside leading to Derby. The last occupant had been a Mr Clavering – a Northumberland gentleman of good family – who had come to live in Barford while he was but a younger son; but when some elder branches of the family died, he had returned to take possession of the family estate. The house of which I speak was called the White House, from its being covered with a greyish kind of stucco. It had a good garden to the back, and Mr Clavering had built capital stables, with what were then considered the latest improvements. The point of good stabling was expected to let the house, as it was in a hunting county; otherwise it had few recommendations. There were many bedrooms; some entered through others, even to the number of five, leading one beyond the other; several sitting rooms of the small and poky kind, wainscotted round with wood, and then painted a heavy slate colour; one good dining room, and a drawing room over it, both looking into the garden, with pleasant bow windows.

Such was the accommodation offered by the White House. It did not seem to be very tempting to strangers, though the good people of Barford rather piqued themselves on it, as the largest house in the town; and as a house in which 'towns-people' and 'county people' had often met at Mr Clavering's friendly dinners. To appreciate this circumstance of pleasant recollection, you should have lived some years in a little country town, surrounded by gentlemen's seats. You would then understand how a bow or a courtesy from a member of a county family elevates the individuals who receive it almost as much, in their own eyes, as the pair of blue garters fringed with silver did Mr Bickerstaff's ward.[35] They trip lightly on air for a whole day afterwards. Now Mr Clavering was gone, where could town and county mingle?

I mention these things that you may have an idea of the desirability of the letting of the White House in the Barfordites' imagination; and to make the mixture thick and slab,[36] you must add for yourselves the bustle, the mystery, and the importance which every little event either causes or assumes in a small town; and then, perhaps, it will be no wonder to you that twenty ragged little urchins accompanied 'the gentleman' aforesaid to the door of the White House; and that, although he was above an hour inspecting it under the auspices of Mr Jones, the agent's clerk, thirty more had joined themselves on to the wondering crowd before his exit, and awaited such crumbs of intelligence as they could gather before they were threatened or whipped out of hearing distance. Presently out came 'the gentleman' and the lawyer's clerk. The latter was speaking as he followed the former over the threshold. The gentleman was tall, well dressed, handsome; but there was a sinister cold look in his quick-glancing, light blue eye, which a keen observer might not have liked. There were no keen observers among the boys, and ill-conditioned gaping girls. But they stood too near; inconveniently close; and the gentleman, lifting up his right hand, in which he carried a short riding whip, dealt one or two sharp blows to the nearest, with a look of savage enjoyment on his face as they moved away whimpering and crying. An instant after, his expression of countenance had changed.

'Here!' said he, drawing out a handful of money, partly silver, partly copper, and throwing it into the midst of them. 'Scramble for it! fight it out, my lads! come this afternoon, at three, to the George, and I'll throw you out some more.' So the boys hurrahed for him as he walked off with the agent's clerk. He chuckled to himself, as over a pleasant thought. 'I'll have some fun with those lads,' he said; 'I'll teach 'em to come prowling and prying about me. I'll tell you what I'll do. I'll make the money so hot in the fire shovel that it shall burn their fingers. You come and see the faces and the howling. I shall be very glad if you will dine with me at two; and by that time I may have made up my mind respecting the house.'

Mr Jones, the agent's clerk, agreed to come to the George at two, but, somehow, he had a distaste for his entertainer. Mr Jones would not like to have said, even to himself, that a man with a purse full of money, who kept many horses, and spoke familiarly of noblemen – above all, who thought of taking the White House – could be anything but a gentleman; but still the uneasy wonder as to who this Mr Robinson Higgins could be, filled the clerk's mind long after Mr Higgins, Mr Higgins' servants, and Mr Higgins' stud had taken possession of the White House.

The White House was re-stuccoed (this time of a pale yellow colour), and put into thorough repair by the accom-modating and delighted landlord; while his tenant seemed inclined to spend any amount of money on internal decora-tions, which were showy and effective in their character, enough to make the White House a nine days' wonder to the good people of Barford. The slate-coloured paints became pink, and were picked out with gold; the old-fashioned bannisters were replaced by newly gilt ones; but, above all, the stables were a sight to be seen. Since the days of the Roman

Emperor never was there such provision made for the care, the comfort, and the health of horses.[37] But everyone said it was no wonder, when they were led through Barford, covered up to their eyes, but curving their arched and delicate necks, and prancing with short high steps, in repressed eagerness. Only one groom came with them; yet they required the care of three men. Mr Higgins, however, preferred engaging two lads out of Barford; and Barford highly approved of his preference. Not only was it kind and thoughtful to give employment to the lounging lads themselves, but they were receiving such a training in Mr Higgins's stables as might fit them for Doncaster or Newmarket.[38] The district of Derbyshire in which Barford was situated, was too close to Leicestershire not to support a hunt and a pack of hounds. The master of the hounds was a certain Sir Harry Manley, who was *aut nullus*. He measured a man by the 'length of his fork', not by the expression of his countenance, or the shape of his head.[39] But as Sir Henry was wont to observe, there was such a thing as too long a fork, so his approbation was withheld until he had seen a man on horseback; and if his seat there was square and easy, his hand light, and his courage good, Sir Harry hailed him as a brother.

Mr Higgins attended the first meet of the season, not as a subscriber but as an amateur. The Barford Huntsmen piqued themselves on their bold riding; and their knowledge of the country came by nature; yet this new strange man, whom nobody knew, was in at the death, sitting on his horse, both well breathed and calm, without a hair turned on the sleek skin of the latter, supremely addressing the old huntsman as he hacked off the tail of the fox; and he, the old man, who was testy even under Sir Harry's slightest rebuke, and flew out on any other member of the hunt that dared to utter a word against his sixty years' experience as stable boy, groom, poacher, and what not – he, old Isaac Wormeley, was meekly listening to the wisdom of this stranger, only now and then giving one of his quick, upturning, cunning glances, not unlike the sharp o'er-canny looks of the poor deceased Reynard, round whom the hounds were howling, unadmonished by the short whip, which was now tucked into Wormeley's well-worn pocket. When Sir Harry rode into the copse – full of dead brushwood and wet tangled grass – and was followed by the members of the hunt, as one by one they cantered past, Mr Higgins took off his cap and bowed – half deferentially, half insolently – with a lurking smile in the corner of his eye at the discomfited looks of one or two of the laggards. 'A famous run, sir,' said Sir Harry. 'The first time you have hunted in our country, but I hope we shall see you often.'

'I hope to become a member of the hunt, sir,' said Mr Higgins.

'Most happy – proud, I'm sure, to receive so daring a rider among us. You took the Cropper-gate, I fancy; while some of our friends here' – scowling at one or two cowards by way of finishing his speech. 'Allow me to introduce myself – master of the hounds,' he fumbled in his waistcoat pocket for the card on which his name was formally inscribed. 'Some of our friends here are kind enough to come home with me to dinner; might I ask for the honour?'

'My name is Higgins,' replied the stranger, bowing low. 'I am only lately come to occupy the White House at Barford, and I have not as yet presented my letters of introduction.'

'Hang it!' replied Sir Harry; 'a man with a seat like yours, and that good brush in your hand, might ride up to any door in the county (I'm a Leicestershire man!), and be a welcome guest. Mr Higgins, I shall be proud to become better acquainted with you over my dinner table.'

Mr Higgins knew pretty well how to improve the acquaintance thus begun. He could sing a good song, tell a good story, and was well up in practical jokes; with plenty of that keen wordly sense, which seems like an instinct in some men, and which in this case taught him on whom he might play off such jokes, with impunity from their resentment, and with a security of applause from the more boisterous, vehement, or prosperous. At the end of twelve months Mr Robinson Higgins was, out-and-out, the most popular member of Barford hunt; had beaten all the others by a couple of lengths, as his first patron, Sir Harry, observed one evening, when they were just leaving the dinner table of an old hunting squire in the neighbourhood.

'Because, you know,' said Squire Hearn, holding Sir Harry by the button – 'I mean, you see, this young spark is looking sweet upon Catherine; and she's a good girl, and will have ten thousand pounds down the day she's married, by her mother's will; and – excuse me, Sir Harry – but I should not like my girl to throw herself away.'

Though Sir Harry had a long ride before him, and but the early and short light of a new moon to take it in, his kind heart was so much touched by Squire Hearn's trembling tearful anxiety, that he stopped, and turned back into the dining room to say, with more asseverations than I care to give:

'My good Squire, I may say, I know that man pretty well by this time; and a better fellow never existed. If I had twenty daughters, he should have the pick of them.'

Squire Hearn never thought of asking the grounds for his old friend's opinion of Mr Higgins; it had been given with too much earnestness for any doubts to cross the old man's mind as to the possibility of its not being well founded. Mr Hearn was not a doubter or a thinker, or suspicious by nature; it was simply his love for Catherine, his only child,[40] that prompted his anxiety in this case; and, after what Sir Harry had said, the old man could totter with an easy mind, though not with very steady legs, into the drawing room, where his bonny blushing daughter Catherine and Mr Higgins stood close together on the hearthrug – he whispering, she listening with downcast eyes. She looked so happy, so like her dead mother had looked when the Squire was a young man, that all his thought was how to please her most. His son and heir was about to be married, and bring his wife to live with the Squire; Barford and the White House were not distant an hour's ride; and, even as these thoughts passed through his mind, he asked Mr Higgins if he could not stay all night – the young moon was already set – the roads would be dark – and Catherine looked up with a pretty anxiety, which, however, had not much doubt in it, for the answer.

With every encouragement of this kind from the old Squire, it took everybody rather by surprise when one morning it was discovered that Miss Catherine Hearn was missing; and when, according to the usual fashion in such cases, a note was found, saying that she had eloped with 'the man of her heart', and gone to Gretna Green,[41] no one could imagine why she could not quietly have stopped at home and been married in the parish church. She had always been a romantic, sentimental girl; very pretty and very affectionate, and very much spoiled, and very much wanting in common sense. Her indulgent father was deeply hurt at this want of confidence in his never-varying affection; but when his son came, hot with indignation from the Baronet's (his future father-in-law's house, where every form of law and of ceremony was to accompany his own impending marriage), Squire Hearn pleaded the cause of the young couple with imploring cogency, and protested that it was a piece of spirit in his daughter, which he admired and was proud of. However, it ended with Mr Nathaniel Hearn's declaring that he and his wife would have nothing to do with his sister and her husband. 'Wait till you've seen him, Nat!' said the old Squire, trembling with his distressful anticipations of family discord, 'He's an excuse for any girl. Only ask Sir Harry's opinion of him.'

'Confound Sir Harry! So that a man sits his horse well, Sir Harry cares nothing about anything else. Who is this man – this fellow? Where does he come from? What are his means? Who are his family?'

'He comes from the south – Surrey or Somersetshire, I forget which; and he pays his way well and liberally. There's not a tradesman in Barford but says he cares no more for money than for water; he spends like a prince, Nat. I don't know who his family are, but he seals with a coat of arms which may tell you if you want to know – and he goes regularly to collect his rents from his estates in the south. Oh, Nat! if you would but be friendly, I should be as well pleased with Kitty's marriage as any father in the county.'

Mr Nathaniel Hearn gloomed, and muttered an oath or two to himself. The poor old father was reaping the consequences of his weak indulgence to his two children. Mr and Mrs Nathaniel Hearn kept apart from Catherine and her husband; and Squire Hearn durst never ask them to Levison Hall, though it was his own house. Indeed, he stole away as if he were a culprit whenever he went to visit the White House; and if he passed a night there, he was fain to equivocate when he returned home the next day; an equivocation which was well interpreted by the surly proud Nathaniel. But the younger Mr and Mrs Hearn were the only people who did not visit at the White House. Mr and Mrs Higgins were decidedly more popular than their brother and sister-in-law. She made a very pretty sweet-tempered hostess, and her education had not been such as to make her intolerant of any want of refinement in the associates who gathered round her husband. She had gentle smiles for townspeople as well as county people; and unconsciously played an admirable second in her husband's project of making himself universally popular.

But there is someone to make ill-natured remarks, and draw ill-natured conclusions from very simple premises, in every place; and in Barford this bird of ill omen was a Miss Pratt. She did not hunt – so Mr Higgins' admirable riding did not call out her admiration. She did not drink – so the well-selected wines, so lavishly dispensed among his guests, could never mollify Miss Pratt. She could not bear comic songs, or buffo stories – so, in that way, her approbation was impregnable. And these three secrets of popularity constituted Mr Higgins' great charm. Miss Pratt sat and watched. Her face looked immoveably grave at the end of any of Mr Higgins' best stories; but there was a keen needle-like glance of her unwinking little eyes, which Mr Higgins felt rather than saw, and which made him shiver, even on a hot day, when it fell upon him. Miss Pratt was a dissenter, and, to propitiate this female Mordecai,[42] Mr Higgins asked the dissenting minister whose service she attended to dinner; kept himself and his company in good order; gave a handsome donation to the poor of the chapel. All in vain – Miss Pratt stirred not a muscle more of her face towards graciousness; and Mr Higgins was conscious that, in spite of all his open efforts to captivate Mr Davis, there was a secret influence on the other side, throwing in doubts and suspicions, and evil interpretations of all he said or did. Miss Pratt, the little, plain old maid, living on eighty pounds a year, was the thorn in the popular Mr

Higgins' side, although she had never spoken one uncivil word to him; indeed, on the contrary, had treated him with a stiff and elaborate civility.

The thorn – the grief to Mrs Higgins was this. They had no children! Oh! how she would stand and envy the careless busy motion of half-a-dozen children; and then, when observed, move on with a deep, deep sigh of yearning regret. But it was as well.

It was noticed that Mr Higgins was remarkably careful of his health. He ate, drank, took exercise, rested, by some secret rules of his own; occasionally bursting into an excess, it is true, but only on rare occasions – such as when he returned from visiting his estates in the south, and collecting his rents. That unusual exertion and fatigue – for there were no stagecoaches within forty miles of Barford, and he, like most country gentlemen of that day, would have preferred riding if there had been – seemed to require some strange excess to compensate for it; and rumours went through the town, that he shut himself up, and drank enormously for some days after his return. But no one was admitted to these orgies.

One day – they remembered it well afterwards – the hounds met not far from the town; and the fox was found in a part of the wild heath, which was beginning to be enclosed by a few of the more wealthy townspeople, who were desirous of building themselves houses rather more in the country than those they had hitherto lived in. Among these, the principal was a Mr Dudgeon, the attorney of Barford, and the agent for all the county families about. The firm of Dudgeon had managed the leases, the marriage settlements, and the wills, of the neighbourhood for generations. Mr Dudgeon's father had the responsibility of collecting the landowners' rents just as the present Mr Dudgeon had at the time of which I speak: and as his son and his son's son have done since. Their business was an hereditary estate to them; and with something of the old feudal feeling, was mixed a kind of proud humility at their position towards the squires whose family secrets they had mastered, and the mysteries of whose fortunes and estates were better known to the Messrs Dudgeon than to themselves.

Mr John Dudgeon had built himself a house on Wildbury Heath; a mere cottage, as he called it: but though only two stories high, it spread out far and wide, and workpeople from Derby had been sent for on purpose to make the inside as complete as possible. The gardens too were exquisite in arrangement, if not very extensive; and not a flower was grown in them but of the rarest species. It must have been somewhat of a mortification to the owner of this dainty place when, on the day of which I speak, the fox after a long race, during which he had described a circle of many miles, took refuge in the garden; but Mr Dudgeon put a good face on the matter when a gentleman hunter, with the careless insolence of the squires of those days and that place, rode across the velvet lawn, and tapping at the window of the dining room with his whip handle, asked permission – no! that is not it – rather, informed Mr Dudgeon of their intention – to enter his garden in a body, and have the fox unearthed. Mr Dudgeon compelled himself to smile assent, with the grace of a masculine Griselda;[43] and then he hastily gave orders to have all that the house afforded of provision set out for luncheon, guessing rightly enough that a six hours' run would give even homely fare an acceptable welcome. He bore without wincing the entrance of the dirty boots into his exquisitely clean rooms; he only felt grateful for the care with which Mr Higgins strode about, laboriously and noiselessly moving on the tip of his toes, as he reconnoitred the rooms with a curious eye.

'I'm going to build a house myself, Dudgeon; and, upon my word, I don't think I could take a better model than yours.'

'Oh! my poor cottage would be too small to afford any hints for such a house as you would wish to build, Mr Higgins,' replied Mr Dudgeon, gently rubbing his hands nevertheless at the compliment.

'Not at all! not at all! Let me see. You have dining room, drawing room' – he hesitated, and Mr Dudgeon filled up the blank as he expected.

'Four sitting rooms and the bedrooms. But allow me to show you over the house. I confess I took some pains in arranging it, and, though far smaller than what you would require, it may, nevertheless, afford you some hints.'

So they left the eating gentlemen with their mouths and their plates quite full, and the scent of the fox overpowering that of the hasty rashers of ham; and they carefully inspected all the ground-floor rooms. Then Mr Dudgeon said:

'If you are not tired, Mr Higgins – it is rather my hobby, so you must pull me up if you are – we will go upstairs, and I will show you my sanctum.'

Mr Dudgeon's sanctum was the centre room, over the porch, which formed a balcony, and which was carefully filled with choice flowers in pots. Inside, there were all kinds of elegant contrivances for hiding the real strength of all the boxes and chests required by the particular nature of Mr Dudgeon's business; for although his office was in Barford, he kept (as he informed Mr Higgins) what was the most valuable here, as being safer than an office which was locked up and left every night. But, as Mr Higgins reminded him with a sly poke in the side, when next they met, his own house was not over-secure. A fortnight after the gentlemen of the Barford hunt lunched there, Mr Dudgeon's strongbox, – in his sanctum upstairs, with the mysterious spring-bolt to the window invented by himself, and the secret of which was only known to the inventor and a few of his most intimate friends, to whom he had proudly shown it; – this strongbox, containing the collected Christmas rents of half-a-dozen landlords, (there was then no bank nearer than Derby,) was rifled; and the secretly rich Mr Dudgeon had to stop his agent in his purchases of paintings by Flemish artists, because the money was required to make good the missing rents.

The Dogberries and Verges[44] of those days were quite incapable of obtaining any clue to the robber or robbers; and though one or two vagrants were taken up and brought before Mr Dunover and Mr Higgins, the magistrates who usually attended in the courtroom at Barford, there was no evidence brought against them, and after a couple of nights' durance in the lock-ups they were set at liberty. But it became a standing joke with Mr Higgins to ask Mr Dudgeon, from time to time, whether he could recommend him a place of safety for his valuables; or, if he had made any more inventions lately for securing houses from robbers.

About two years after this time – about seven years after Mr Higgins had been married – one Tuesday evening, Mr Davis was sitting reading the news in the coffee room of the George Inn. He belonged to a club of gentlemen who met there occasionally to play at whist, to read what few newspapers and magazines were published in those days, to chat about the market at Derby, and prices all over the country. This Tuesday night, it was a black frost; and few people were in the room. Mr Davis was anxious to finish an article in the *Gentleman's Magazine*; indeed, he was making extracts from it, intending to answer it, and yet unable with his small income to purchase a copy. So he staid late; it was past nine, and at ten o'clock the room was closed. But while he wrote, Mr Higgins came in. He was pale and haggard with cold; Mr Davis, who had had for some time sole possession of the fire, moved politely on one side, and handed to the newcomer the sole London newspaper which the room afforded. Mr Higgins accepted it, and made some remark on the intense coldness of the weather; but Mr Davis was too full of his article, and intended reply, to fall into conversation readily. Mr Higgins hitched his chair nearer to the fire, and put his feet on the fender, giving an audible shudder. He put the newspaper on one end of the table near him, and sat gazing into the red embers of the fire, crouching down over them as if his very marrow were chilled. At length he said:

'There is no account of the murder at Bath in that paper?' Mr Davis, who had finished taking his notes, and was preparing to go, stopped short, and asked:

'Has there been a murder at Bath? No! I have not seen anything of it – who was murdered?'

'Oh! it was a shocking, terrible murder!' said Mr Higgins not raising his look from the fire, but gazing on with his eyes dilated till the whites were seen all round them. 'A terrible, terrible murder! I wonder what will become of the murderer? I can fancy the red glowing centre of that fire – look and see how infinitely distant it seems, and how the distance magnifies it into something awful and unquenchable.'

'My dear sir, you are feverish; how you shake and shiver!' said Mr Davis, thinking privately that his companion had symptoms of fever, and that he was wandering in his mind.

'Oh, no!' said Mr Higgins. 'I am not feverish. It is the night which is so cold.' And for a time he talked with Mr Davis about the article in the *Gentleman's Magazine*, for he was rather a reader himself, and could take more interest in Mr

Davis' pursuits than most of the people at Barford. At length it drew near to ten, and Mr Davis rose up to go home to his lodgings.

'No, Davis, don't go. I want you here. We will have a bottle of port together, and that will put Saunders into good humour. I want to tell you about this murder,' he continued, dropping his voice, and speaking hoarse and low. 'She was an old woman, and he killed her, sitting reading her Bible by her own fireside!' He looked at Mr Davis with a strange searching gaze, as if trying to find some sympathy in the horror which the idea presented to him.

'Who do you mean, my dear sir? What is this murder you are so full of? No one has been murdered here.'

'No, you fool! I tell you it was in Bath!' said Mr Higgins, with sudden passion; and then calming himself to most velvet-smoothness of manner, he laid his hand on Mr Davis' knee, there, as they sat by the fire, and gently detaining him, began the narration of the crime he was so full of; but his voice and manner were constrained to a stony quietude; he never looked in Mr Davis' face; once or twice, as Mr Davis remembered afterwards, his grip tightened like a compressing vice.

'She lived in a small house in a quiet old-fashioned street, she and her maid. People said she was a good old woman; but for all that she hoarded and hoarded, and never gave to the poor. Mr Davis, it is wicked not to give to the poor – wicked – wicked, is it not? I always give to the poor, for once I read in the Bible that "Charity covereth a multitude of sins".[45] The wicked old woman never gave, but hoarded her money, and saved, and saved. Someone heard of it; I say she threw a temptation in his way, and God will punish her for it. And this man – or it might be a woman, who knows? – and this person – heard also that she went to church in the mornings, and her maid in the afternoons; and so – while the maid was at church, and the street and the house quite still, and the darkness of a winter afternoon coming on – she was nodding over the Bible – and that, mark you! is a sin, and one that God will avenge sooner or later; and a step came in the dusk up the stair, and that person I told you of stood in the room. At first he – no! At first, it is supposed – for, you understand, all this is mere guess work – it is supposed that he asked her civilly enough to give him her money, or to tell him where it was; but the old miser defied him, and would not ask for mercy and give up her keys, even when he threatened her, but looked him in the face as if he had been a baby – Oh, God! Mr Davis, I once dreamt when I was a little innocent boy that I should commit a crime like this, and I wakened up crying; and my mother comforted me – that is the reason I tremble so now – that and the cold, for it is very very cold!'

'But did he murder the old lady?' asked Mr Davis. 'I beg your pardon, sir, but I am interested by your story.'

'Yes! he cut her throat; and there she lies yet in her quiet little parlour, with her face upturned and all ghastly white, in the middle of a pool of blood. Mr Davis, this wine is no better than water; I must have some brandy!'

Mr Davis was horror-struck by the story, which seemed to have fascinated him as much as it had done his companion.

'Have they got any clue to the murderer?' said he. Mr Higgins drank down half a tumbler of raw brandy before he answered.

'No! no clue whatever. They will never be able to discover him, and I should not wonder – Mr Davis – I should not wonder if he repented after all, and did bitter penance for his crime; and if so – will there be mercy for him at the last day?'

'God knows!' said Mr Davis, with solemnity. 'It is an awful story,' continued he, rousing himself; 'I hardly like to leave this warm light room and go out into the darkness after hearing it. But it must be done,' buttoning on his greatcoat – 'I can only say I hope and trust they will find out the murderer and hang him. If you'll take my advice, Mr Higgins, you'll have your bed warmed, and drink a treacle-posset just the last thing; and, if you'll allow me, I'll send you my answer to Philologus before it goes up to old Urban.'[46]

The next morning Mr Davis went to call on Miss Pratt, who was not very well; and by way of being agreeable and entertaining, he related to her all he had heard the night before about the murder at Bath; and really he made a very pretty connected story out of it, and interested Miss Pratt very much in the fate of the old lady – partly because of a similarity in their situations; for she also privately hoarded money, and had but one servant, and stopped at home alone on Sunday afternoons to allow her servant to go to church.

'And when did all this happen?' she asked.

'I don't know if Mr Higgins named the day; and yet I think it must have been on this very last Sunday.'

'And today is Wednesday. Ill news travels fast.'

'Yes, Mr Higgins thought it might have been in the London newspaper.'

'That it could never be. Where did Mr Higgins learn all about it?'

'I don't know, I did not ask; I think he only came home yesterday: he had been south to collect his rents, somebody said.'

Miss Pratt grunted. She used to vent her dislike and suspicions of Mr Higgins in a grunt whenever his name was mentioned.

'Well, I shan't see you for some days. Godfrey Merton has asked me to go and stay with him and his sister; and I think it will do me good. Besides,' added she, 'these winter evenings – and these murderers at large in the country – I don't quite like living with only Peggy to call to in case of need.'

Miss Pratt went to stay with her cousin, Mr Merton. He was an active magistrate, and enjoyed his reputation as such. One day he came in, having just received his letters.

'Bad account of the morals of your little town here, Jessy!' said he, touching one of his letters. 'You've either a murderer among you, or some friend of a murderer. Here's a poor old lady at Bath had her throat cut last Sunday week; and I've a letter from the Home Office, asking to lend them "my very efficient aid", as they are pleased to call it, towards finding out the culprit. It seems he must have been thirsty, and of a comfortable jolly turn; for before going to his horrid work he tapped a barrel of ginger wine the old lady had set by to work; and he wrapped the spigot round with a piece of a letter taken out of his pocket, as may be supposed; and this piece of a letter was found afterwards; there are only these letters on the outside: "*ns, Esq., –arford, –egworth*", which someone has ingeniously made out to mean Barford, near Kegworth. On the other side there is some allusion to a racehorse, I conjecture, though the name is singular enough: "Church-and-King-and-down-with-the-Rump."'[47]

Miss Pratt caught at this name immediately; it had hurt her feelings as a dissenter only a few months ago, and she remembered it well.

'Mr Nat Hearn has – or had (as I am speaking in the witness box, as it were, I must take care of my tenses), a horse with that ridiculous name.'

'Mr Nat Hearn,' repeated Mr Merton, making a note of the intelligence; then he recurred to his letter from the Home Office again.

'There is also a piece of a small key, broken in the futile attempt to open a desk – well, well. Nothing more of consequence. The letter is what we must rely upon.'

'Mr Davis said that Mr Higgins told him – ' Miss Pratt began.

'Higgins!' exclaimed Mr Merton, '*ns*. Is it Higgins, the blustering fellow that ran away with Nat Hearn's sister?'

'Yes!' said Miss Pratt. 'But though he has never been a favourite of mine – '

'*ns*.' repeated Mr Merton. 'It is too horrible to think of; a member of the hunt – kind old Squire Hearn's son-in-law! Who else have you in Barford with names that end with *ns*?'

'There's Jackson, and Higginson, and Blenkinsop, and Davis and Jones. Cousin! One thing strikes me – how did Mr Higgins know all about it to tell Mr Davis on Tuesday what had happened on Sunday afternoon?'

There is no need to add much more. Those curious in lives of the highwaymen may find the name of Higgins as conspicuous among those annals as that of Claude Duval.[48] Kate Hearn's husband collected his rents on the highway, like many another 'gentleman' of the day; but, having been unlucky in one or two of his adventures, and hearing exaggerated accounts of the hoarded wealth of the old lady at Bath, he was led on from robbery to murder, and was hung for his crime at Derby, in seventeen hundred and seventy-five.

He had not been an unkind husband; and his poor wife took lodgings in Derby to be near him in his last moments – his awful last moments. Her old father went with her everywhere but into her husband's cell; and wrung her heart by constantly accusing himself of having promoted her marriage with a man of whom he knew so little. He abdicated his squireship in favour of his son Nathaniel. Nat was prosperous, and the helpless silly father could be of no use to him; but to his widowed daughter the foolish fond old man was all in all; her knight, her protector, her companion – her most faithful loving companion. Only he ever declined assuming the office of her counsellor – shaking his head sadly, and saying –

'Ah! Kate, Kate! if I had had more wisdom to have advised thee better, thou need'st not have been an exile here in Brussels, shrinking from the sight of every English person as if they knew thy story.'

I saw the White House not a month ago; it was to let, perhaps for the twentieth time since Mr Higgins occupied it; but still the tradition goes in Barford that once upon a time a highwayman lived there, and amassed untold treasures; and that the ill-gotten wealth yet remains walled up in some unknown concealed chamber; but in what part of the house no one knows.

Will any of you become tenants, and try to find out this mysterious closet? I can furnish the exact address to any applicant who wishes for it.

UNCLE GEORGE'S STORY
[by Edmund Saul Dixon and W.H. Wills]

We had devoted the morning before my wedding day to the arrangement of those troublesome, delightful, endless little affairs, which the world says must be set in order on such occasions; and late in the afternoon, we walked down, Charlotte and myself, to take a last bachelor and maiden peep at the home which, next day, was to be ours in partnership. Goody Barnes, already installed as our cook and house-keeper, stood at the door, ready to receive us as we crossed the marketplace to inspect our cottage for the twentieth time – cottage by courtesy – next door to my father's mansion, by far the best and handsomest in the place. It was some distance from Charlotte's house, where she and her widowed mother lived; – all the way down the lime tree avenue, then over the breezy common, besides traversing the principal and only street, which terminated in the village marketplace.

The front of our house was Quaker-like, in point of neat-ness and humility. But enter! It is not hard to display good taste when the banker's book puts no veto on the choice gems of furniture, which give the finishing touch to the whole. Then pass through, and bestow a glance upon our living rooms looking down upon that greatest of luxuries, a terraced garden, commanding the country – and not a little of that country mine already, – the farm which my father had given me, to keep me quiet and contented at home. For the closing perspective of our view, there was the sea, like a bright blue rampart rising before us. White-sailed vessels, or self-willed steamers, flitted to and fro for our amusement.

We tripped down the terrace steps, and of course looked in upon the little artificial grotto to the right, which I had caused to be lined throughout with foreign shells and glittering spars[49] – more gifts from my ever-bountiful father. Charlotte and I went laughingly along the straight gravel walk, flanked on each side with a regiment of dahlias; that led us to the little gate, opening to give us admission to my father's own pleasure ground and orchard.

The dear old man was rejoiced to receive us. A daughter was what he so long had wished for. We hardly knew whether to smile, or weep for joy, as we all sat together on the same rustic bench, overshadowed by the tulip tree, which someone said my father had himself brought from North America. But of the means by which he became possessed of many of his choicest treasures, he never breathed a syllable to me. His father, I very well knew, was nothing more than a homely farmer, cultivating no great extent of not too productive seaside land; but Charlotte's lace dress which she was to wear tomorrow – again another present from him – was, her mother proudly pronounced, valuable and handsome enough for a princess.

Charlotte half whispered, half said aloud that she had no fear now that Richard Leroy, her boisterous admirer, would dare to attempt his reported threat to carry her off to the continent in his cutter.[50] Richard's name made my father frown, so we said no more; we lapsed again into that dreamy state of silent enjoyment, which was the best expression of our happiness.

Leroy's father was *called* a farmer; but on our portion of the English coast there are many things that are well understood rather than clearly and distinctly expressed; and no one had ever enlightened my ignorance. My father was on speaking terms with him, that was all; courteous, but distant; half timid, half mysterious. He discouraged my childish intimacy with

Richard; yet he did not go so far as to forbid it. Once, when I urged him to allow me to accompany young Leroy in his boat, to fish in the Channel one calm and bright summer morning, he peremptorily answered, 'No! I do not wish *you* to learn to be a smuggler.' But then, he instantly checked himself, and afterwards was more anxious and kind to me than ever. Still Richard and I continued playfellows until we grew up, and both admired Charlotte. He would have made a formal proposal for her hand, if the marked discouragement of her family had not shut out every opportunity. This touched his pride, and once made him declare, in an offhand way, that it would cost him but very little trouble to land such a light cargo as that, some pleasant evening, in France, or even on one of the Azore Islands,[51] if orange groves and orange blossoms were what my lady cared about. It is wonderful how far, and how swiftly, heedless words do fly when once they are uttered. Such speeches did not close the breach, but instead, laid the first foundation for one of those confirmed estrangements which village neighbourhoods only know. The repugnance manifested by Charlotte's friends was partly caused by the mystery which hung to Richard's ample means. The choice was unhesitatingly made in my favour. In consequence, as a sort of rejected candidate, Richard Leroy really did lie, amongst us, under an unexpressed and indefinite ban, which was by no means likely to be removed by the roystering,[52] scornful air of superiority with which he mostly spoke of, looked at, and treated us.

Charlotte and I took leave of my father on that grey September evening with the full conviction that every blessing was in store for us which affection and wealth had the power to procure. Over the green, and up the lime tree avenue, and then, goodnight, my lady-love! Goodnight, thus parting for the very last time. Tomorrow – ah! think of tomorrow. The quarters of the church clock strike half-past nine. Goodnight, dear mother-in-law. And, once more, goodnight, Charlotte!

It was somewhat early to leave; but my father's plans required it. He desired that we should be married, not at the church of the village where we all resided, but at one distant a short walk, in which he took a peculiar interest – where he had selected the spot for a family burial place, and where he wished the family registers to be kept. It was a secluded hamlet; and my father had simply made the request that I would lodge for a while at a farmhouse there, in order that the wedding might be performed at the place he fixed his heart upon. My duty and my interest were to obey.

'Goodnight, Charlotte,' had not long been uttered, before I was fairly on the way to my temporary home. Our village, and its few scattered lights, were soon left behind, and I then was upon the open down, walking on with a springing step. On one side was spread the English Channel; and from time to time I could mark the appearance of the light at Cape Grinez, on the French coast opposite. There it was, coming and going, flashing out and dying away, with never-ceasing coquetry. The cliff lay between my path and the sea. There was no danger; for, although the moon was not up, it was bright starlight. I knew every inch of the way as well as I did my father's garden walks. In September, however, mists will rise; and, as I approached the valley, there came the offspring of the pretty stream which ran through it, something like a light cloud running along the ground before the wind. Is there a night fog coming on? Perhaps there may be. If so, better steer quite clear of the cliff, by means of a gentle circuit inland. It is quite impossible to miss the valley; and, once in the valley, it is equally difficult to miss the hamlet. Richard

Leroy has been frequently backward and forward the last few evenings: it would be strange if we should chance to meet here, and on such an occasion.

On, and still on, cheerily. In a few minutes more I shall reach the farm, and then, to pass one more solitary night is almost a pleasurable delay, a refinement in happiness. I could sing and dance for joy. Yes, dance all alone, on this elastic turf! There: just one foolish caper; just one –

Good God! is this not the shock of an earthquake? I hasten to advance another step, but the ground beneath me quivers and sinks. I grasp at the side of a yawning pitfall, but grasp in vain. Down, down, down, I fall headlong.

When my senses returned, and I could look about me, the moon had risen, and was shining in at the treacherous hole through which I had fallen. A glance was only too sufficient to explain my position. Why had I always so foolishly refused to allow the farmer to meet me halfway, and accompany me to his house every evening; knowing, as I did know, how the chalk and limestone of the district had been undermined in catacombs, sinuous and secret for wells, flint, manure, building materials, and worse purposes? My poor father and Charlotte!

Patience. It can hardly be possible that now, on the eve of my marriage, I am suddenly doomed to a lingering death. The night *must* be passed here, and daylight will show some means of escape. I will lie down on this heap of earth that fell under me.

Amidst despairing thoughts, and a hideous waking nightmare, daylight slowly came.

The waning moon had not revealed the extremity of my despair; but now it was clearly visible that I had fallen double the height I supposed. But for the turf which had fallen under me, I must have been killed on the spot. The hole was too large for me to creep up, by pressing against it with my back and knees; and there were no friendly knobs or protuberances visible up its smooth sides. The chasm increased in diameter as it descended, like an inverted funnel. I might possibly climb up a wall; but could I creep along a ceiling?

I shouted as I lay; no one answered. I shouted again – and again. Then I thought that too much shouting would exhaust my strength, and unfit me for the task of mounting. I measured with my eye the distances from stratum to stratum of each well-marked layer of chalk. And then, the successive beds of flint – they gave me the greatest hopes. If foot holes could be only cut! Though the feat was difficult, it might be practicable. The attempt must be made.

I arose, stiff and bruised. No matter. The first layer of flints was not more than seven or eight feet overhead. Those once reached, I could secure a footing, and obtain a first starting place for escape. I tried to climb to them with my feet and hands. Impossible; the crumbling wall would not support half my weight. As fast as I attempted to get handhold or footing, it fell in fragments to the ground.

But, a better thought – to dig it away, and make a mound so high that, by standing on it, I could manage to reach the flint with my hands. I had my knife to help me; and, after much hard work, my object was accomplished, and I got within reach of the shelf.

My hands had firm hold of the horizontal flint. They were cut with clinging; but I found that, by raising myself, and then thrusting my feet into the chalk and marl,[53] I could support myself with one hand only, leaving the other free to work. I did work; clearing away the chalk above the flint, so as to give me greater standing room. At last, I thought I might venture upon the ledge itself. By a supreme effort, I reached the shelf; but moisture had made the chalk unctuous and slippery to the baffled grasp. It was in vain to think of mounting higher, with no point of support, no firm footing. A desperate leap across the chasm afforded not the slightest hope; because, even if successful, I could not for one moment maintain the advantage gained. I was determined to remain on the ledge of flint. Another moment, and a rattling on the floor soon taught me my powerlessness. Down sunk the chalk beneath my weight; and the stony table fell from its fixture, only just failing to crush me under it.

Stunned and cut, and bruised, I spent some time prostrated by half-conscious but acute sensations of misery. Sleep, which as yet I had not felt, began to steal over me, but could gain no mastery. With each moment of incipient unconsciousness, Charlotte was presented to me, first, in her wedding dress; next, on our terrace beckoning me gaily from the garden below; then, we were walking arm-in-arm in smiling conversation; or seated happily together in my father's library. But the full consciousness which rapidly succeeded presented each moment the hideous truth. It was now broad day; and I realised Charlotte's sufferings. I beheld her awaiting me in her bridal dress; now hastening to the window, and straining her sight over the valley, in the hope of my approach; now stricken down by despair at my absence. My father, too, whose life had been always bound up in mine! These fancies destroyed my power of thought. I felt wild and frenzied. I raved and shouted, and then listened, knowing no answer could come.

But an answer did come: a maddening answer. The sound of bells, dull, dead, and, in my hideous well-hole, just distinguishable. They rang out my marriage peal. Why was I not buried alive when I first fell?

I could have drunk blood, in my thirst, had it been offered to me. Die I must, I felt full well; but let me not die with my mouth in flame! Then came the struggle of sleep; and then fitful, tantalising dreams. Charlotte appeared to me plucking grapes, and dropping them playfully into my mouth; or catching water in the hollow of her hand, from the little cascade in our grotto, and I drank. But hark! drip, drip, and again drip! Is this madness still? No. There must be water oozing somewhere out of the sides of this detested hole. Where the treacherous wall is slimiest, where the green patches are brightest and widest spread on the clammy sides of my living sepulchre, there will be the spot to dig and to search.

Again the knife. Every blow gives a more dead and hollow sound. The chalk dislodged is certainly not moister; but the blade sticks fast into wood – the wood of a cask; something slowly begins to trickle down. It is brandy!

Brandy! shall I taste it? Yet, why not? I did; and soon for a time remembered nothing.

I retained a vivid and excited consciousness up to one precise moment, which might have been marked by a stop-watch, and then all outward things were shut out, as suddenly as if a lamp had been extinguished. A long and utter blank succeeded. I have no further recollection either of the duration of time, or of any bodily suffering. Had I died by alcoholic poison – and it is a miracle the brandy did not kill me – then would have been the end of my actual and conscious existence. My senses were dead. If what happened afterwards had occurred at that time, there would have been no story for you to listen to.

Once more, a burning thirst. Hunger had entirely passed away. I looked up, and all was dark; not even the stars or the cloudy sky were to be seen at the opening of my cavern. A shower of earth and heavy stones fell upon me as I lay. I still was barely awake and conscious, and a groan was the only evidence which escaped me that I had again recovered the use of my senses.

'Halloa! What's that down there?' said a voice, whose tone was familiar to me. I uttered a faint but frantic cry.

I heard a moment's whispering, and the hollow echo of departing footsteps, and then all was still again. The voice overhead once more addressed me.

'Courage, George; keep up your spirits! In two minutes I will come and help you. Don't you know me?'

I then did know that it could be no other than my old rival, Richard Leroy. Before I could collect my thoughts, a light glimmered against one side of the well; and then, in the direction opposite the fallen table of flint, and just over it, Richard appeared, with a lantern in one hand, and a rope tied to a stick across it in the other.

'Have you strength enough left to sit upon this, and to hold by the rope while I haul you up?'

'I think I have,' I said. I got the stick under me, and held by the rope to keep steady on my seat. Richard planted his feet firmly on the edge of his standing place, and hauled me up. By a sleight of hand and an effort of strength, in which I was too weak to render him the least assistance, he landed me at the mouth of a subterranean gallery opening into the well. I could just see, on looking back, that if I had only maintained my position on the ledge of flint, and improved it a little, I might, by a daring and vigorous leap, have sprung to the entrance of this very gallery. But those ideas were now useless. I was so thoroughly worn out that I could scarcely stand, and an entreaty for water preceded even my expression of thanks.

'You shall drink your fill in one instant, and I am heartily glad to have helped you; but first let me mention one thing. It is understood that you keep my secret. You cannot leave this place – unless I blindfold you, which would be an insult – without learning the way to return to it; and, of course, what you see along the galleries are to you nothing but shadows and dreams. Have I your promise?'

I was unable to make any other reply than to seize his hand, and burst into tears. How I got from the caverns to the face of the cliff, how thence to the beach, the secluded hamlet, and the sleeping village, does really seem to my memory like a vision. On the way across the downs, Leroy stopped once or twice, more for the sake of resting my aching limbs, than of taking breath or repose himself. During those intervals, he quietly remarked to me how prejudiced and unfair we had all of us been to him; that as for Charlotte, he considered her as a child, a little sister, almost even as a baby plaything. She was not the woman for him: he, for his part, liked a girl with a little more of the devil about her. No doubt he could have carried her off; and no doubt she would have loved him desperately a fortnight afterwards. But, when he had once got her, what should he have done with such a blue-eyed milk-and-water angel as that? Nothing serious to annoy us had ever entered his head. And my father ought not quite to forget the source of his own fortune, and hold himself aloof from his equals; although he might be lying quiet in harbour at present. Really, it was a joke, that, instead of eloping with the bride, he should be bringing home the eloped bridegroom!

I fainted when he carried me into my father's house, and I remember no more than his temporary adieu. But afterwards, all went on slowly and surely. My father and Richard became good friends, and the old gentleman acquired such influence over him, that Leroy's 'pleasure trips' soon became rare, and finally ceased altogether. At the last run, he brought a foreign wife over with him, and nothing besides – a Dutchwoman of great beauty and accomplishments; who, as he said, was as fitting a helpmate for him, as Charlotte, he acknowledged, was for me. He also took a neighbouring parish church and its appurtenances[54] into favour, and settled down as a landsman within a few miles of us. And, if our families continue to go on in the friendly way they have done for the last few years, it seems likely that a Richard may conduct a Charlotte, to enter their names together in a favourite register book.

THE COLONEL'S STORY
[by Samuel Sidney]

Until I was fifteen I lived at home with my widowed mother and two sisters. My mother was the widow of an officer, who was killed in one of the battles with Hyder Ali,[55] and enjoyed a pension from the Indian Government. I was the youngest; and soon after my fifteenth birthday she died suddenly. My sisters went to India on the invitation of a distant relation of my mother; and I was sent to school, where I was very unhappy. You will, therefore, easily imagine with what pleasure I received a visit from a handsome jovial old gentleman, who told me that he was my father's elder half-brother; that they had been separated by a quarrel early in life, but that now, being a widower and childless, he had found me out, and determined to adopt me.

The truth was, the old man loved company; and that as his chief income – a large one – was derived from a mine, near which he lived, in a very remote part of the country, he was well pleased to have a young companion who looked like a gentleman, and could be useful as carver, cellar keeper, and secretary.

Installed in his house, a room was assigned to me, and I had a servant, and a couple of excellent horses. He made me understand that I need give myself no further anxiety on the subject of my future, that I might abandon the idea of proceeding to India in the Company's service, where a cadetship had been secured for me; and that so long as I conformed to his ways, it was no matter whether I studied or not; in fact, it was no matter what I did.

Some time after becoming thus settled at Beechgrove Hall, my uncle's attacks of gout, in spite of the generous living he adopted as a precaution, became so severe, that he was unable to stir out except in a wheeled chair, and it was with difficulty that he was lifted occasionally into his carriage. The consequence was, that to me all his business naturally fell, and although he grumbled at losing my society and attention, he was obliged to send me to London to watch the progress of a canal bill, in which he was deeply interested. It was my first visit to London. I was well provided with introductions and with funds. My uncle's business occupied me in the morning, for I dreaded his displeasure too much to neglect it; but in the evenings I plunged into every amusement, with all the keen zest of novelty and youth.

I cannot say that up to that period I had never been in love. My uncle had twice seriously warned me that if I made a fool of myself for anything less than a large fortune, he would never forgive me. 'If, Sir,' he said, when, on the second occasion, he saw me blush and tremble – for I was too proud and too self-willed to bear patiently such control – 'If, Sir, you like to make an ass of yourself for a pretty face, like Miss Willington, with her three brothers and five sisters, half of whom you'd have to keep, you may do it with your own money; you shall not do it with mine.'

I told my only confidant, Dr Creeleigh, of this; he answered me, 'You have only about a hundred and twenty a year of your own from the estate you inherited from your father, and you are living with your horses and dogs at the rate of five hundred a year. How would you like to see your wife and children dressed and housed like the curate – poor Mr Serge? Your uncle can't live forever.' The argument was enough for me, who had only found Clara Willington the best partner in country dance. My time was not come.

My lodgings in London were in a large, old-fashioned house in Westminster – formerly the residence of a nobleman –

which was a perfect caravanserai,[56] in the number and variety of its inmates. The best rooms were let to Members of Parliament and persons like myself; but, in the upper floor, many persons of humbler means but genteel pretensions had rooms. Here, I frequently met on the stairs, carrying a roll of music, a tall, elegant female figure, dressed in black, and closely veiled; sometimes, when I had to step on one side, a slight bow was exchanged, but for several weeks that was all. At length my curiosity was piqued; the neat ankles, a small white hand, a dark curl peeping out of the veil, made me anxious to know more.

Enquiries discreetly applied to Mrs Gough, the housekeeper, told me enough to make me wish to know still more. Her name was Laura Delacourt; not more than twenty or twenty-two years of age; she had lived four years previously with her husband in the best apartments in the house in great luxury for one winter. Mr Delacourt was a Frenchman and a gambler; very handsome, and very dissipated; it seemed as if it was her fortune they were spending. Mrs Gough said it was enough to make one's heart break to see that young pretty creature sitting up in her ball dress when her husband had sent her home alone, and remained to play until daylight. They went away, and nothing more was heard of them until just before my arrival. About that time Madame Delacourt, become very humble, had taken a room on the third floor; had only mentioned her husband, to say he was dead, and now apparently lived by giving music lessons.

It would be too long a story to tell how, by making the old housekeeper my ambassador, by anonymous presents of fruit and game, by offering to take music lessons, and by professing to require large quantities of music copied, I made first the acquaintance, and then became the intimate friend of Madame

Delacourt. While keeping me at a freezing distance, and insisting on always having present at our interviews a half-servant half-companion, of that indescribable age, figure, and appearance that is only grown in France, she step by step confided to me her history. An English girl, born in France, the daughter of a war prisoner at Verdun,[57] married to the very handsome Monsieur Delacourt, at sixteen, by a mother who was herself anxious to make a second marriage. In twelve months Monsieur Delacourt had expended her small fortune, and deserted her for an opera dancer of twice her age.

All this, told with a charming accent in melancholy tones – she looking on me sadly with a face which, for expression, I have never seen equalled – produced an impression which those only can understand who have been themselves young and in love.

For weeks this went on, without one sign of encouragement on her part, except that she allowed me to sit with her in the evenings, while her *bonne*[58] faddled at some interminable work, and she sang – O! how divinely! She would receive no presents directly from me; but I sent them anonymously, and dresses and furniture and costly trifles and books reached her daily. I spoke at last; and then she stopped me with a cold faint smile, saying, 'Cease! I must not listen to you.' She pleaded her too recent widowhood, but I persevered; and, after a time, conquered.

She knew my small fortune and large expectations; she knew that our marriage must be a secret; but she was willing to live anywhere, and was well content to quit a life in which she had known so much trouble.

Before the session ended we were married in an obscure church in the City, with no one present but the clerk and the pew-opener. We spent the few following days at a small inn, in a fishing village. Then I had to leave town and carry out the plan I had proposed. I left my wife in lodgings, under an assumed name, at a town within forty miles of our residence. I had some time previously persuaded my uncle to let me take a lease from Lord Mardall of some untouched mineral ground, on very favourable terms, in a wild, thinly peopled district, which was only visited by the gentry for field sports. This afforded me an excuse for being away from home one or two days every week.

Not far from the mines was the remains of a forest, and coverts abounding in game. In a little sloping dell, one of the Lord Mardall's ancestors had built a small shooting lodge, and one of the keepers in charge had planted there fruit trees and ornamental trees, for which he had a taste, being the son of a gardener. On this wild nest, miles away from any other residence, I had fixed my mind. It was half in ruins, and there was no difficulty in obtaining possession. With money and workmen at my command, very soon a garden smiled, and a fountain bubbled at Orchard Spring; roses and climbing plants covered the steep hillside, and the small stone cottage was made, at a slight expense, a wonder of comfort. The cage being ready I brought my bird there. The first months were all joy, all happiness. My uncle only complained that I had lost my jovial spirits.

I counted every day until the day when I could mount my horse and set off for the new mines. Five-and-twenty miles to ride over a rough mountain road; two fords to cross, often swelled by winter rains; but day or night, moonlight or dark, I dashed along, pressing too often my willing horse with loose rein up and down steep hills; all lost in love and anxious thought I rode, until in the distance the plashing sound of the mountain torrent rolling over our garden cascade, told me I was near my darling.

My horse's footsteps were heard, and before I had passed the avenue the door flew open, the bright fire blazed out, and Laura came forward to receive me in her arms.

I had begged her to get everything she might require from London, and have it sent, to avoid all suspicion, to the nearest port, and then brought by her own servant, a country clown, with a horse and cart; and I had given her a cheque book, signed in blank. After a time I saw signs of extravagance; in furniture, in dress, but especially in jewels. I remonstrated gently and was met first with tears; then sullen fits. I learned that Laura had a temper for which I was quite unprepared.

The ice was broken; no more pleasant holydays at Orchard Spring. The girl once so humble now assumed a haughty jealous air; every word was a cause of offence; I never came when wanted, or stayed as long as I was required; half my time was spent in scenes of reproach, of tears, hysterics, lamentations; peace was only to be purchased by some costly present. Our maid-servant, a simple country girl, stood amazed; the meek angel had become a tigress. I loved her still, but feared her; yet even love began to fail before so much violence. A dreadful idea began slowly to intrude itself into my mind. Was she tired of me? Was her story of her life true? Had she ever loved me? The next time that I made up my banker's book I was shocked to find that, in the short time since my last remonstrance, Laura had drawn a large sum of money. I lost no time in galloping to Orchard Spring. She was absent. Where was she? No one knew. Severe cross-examination brought out that she had been away two days; I had not been expected that week. I thought I should have choked.

In the midst I heard the steps of her horse. She came in and confronted me. Looking most beautiful and demoniacal, she defied me; she threatened to expose me to my uncle; declared she had never loved me, but had taken me for a home. At length her frenzy rose to such a height, that she struck me. Then all the violent pent-up rage of my heart broke out. I know not what passed, until I found myself galloping furiously across the mountain ridge that divided the county. Obliged to slacken my pace in passing through a ford, someone spoke to me; how I answered I know not. Whatever it was, it was a mad answer.

I listened to nothing, and pressed on my weary steed until just before reaching the moorland, when, descending into a watercourse, he fell on his head, throwing me over with such force, that for some time I lay senseless. I came to myself to find my poor horse standing over me dead lame. I led him on to the inn door, and knocked. It was midnight, and I was not readily admitted. The landlord, when he saw me, started back with an exclamation of horror. My face and shirt were covered with blood.

Worn-out, bruised, and exhausted by fatigue and passion, I slept. I was rudely awakened, and found myself in the custody of two constables. Two mounted gamekeepers and Lord Mardall had followed and traced me to the inn.

'On what charge?' I asked, amazed.

'For murder,' said Lord Mardall.

'The lady at Orchard Spring,' said one of the gamekeepers.

I was examined before magistrates; but was unable to give any coherent answers; and was committed to the county jail. My uncle remitted me a sum of money for my defence, and desired never to see me again.

I will give you the description of my trial from the newspapers.

The prisoner had clandestinely married a lady of great beauty and unknown family, probably in station beneath himself, and had placed her under an assumed name in a lonely cottage. After a season of affection quarrels had broken out, which, as would be proved by the servant, had constantly increased in violence. On the last occasion when the unfortunate victim was seen alive by her servant, a quarrel of a most fearful description had commenced. It was something about money. The servant had been so much alarmed, that she had left the cottage and gone down to her mother's, a mile away over the hill, where she had previously been ordered to go to obtain some poultry. From something that passed, her mother would not allow her to return. It would then be proved that Lord Mardall, attracted by the howling of a dog, when out shooting the next morning, had entered the open door of the cottage, and had there found the prisoner's wife dead, with a severe fracture of the skull. The prisoner had been pursued, from some information as to his usual course, and found asleep in the chimney corner of the Moor Inn, his clothes and shirt deeply stained with blood. It could be proved that he had washed his face and hands immediately on entering, and attributed the blood to the fall from his horse. But on examination no cuts were found on his person sufficient to cause such an effusion of blood.

But, when Lord Mardall was called, he deposed to two facts which produced a great impression in favour of the prisoner. He saw the body at five o'clock, and it was scarcely cold. He had found in one of the victim's hands a lock of hair, which she had evidently torn from her assailant in her struggles; which had been desperate. He had sealed it up, and never let it out of his possession. The nails of her other hand were broken, and were marked with blood. She had no rings on either of her hands, though she was in the habit of wearing a great number; there were marks of rings, and of one which seemed to have been violently torn off. A packet of plate had been found on the kitchen table, a knife, and a loaf marked with blood.

Counsel were not allowed to address the jury for the defence in those days, and the prisoner was not in a condition to speak on the evidence against him. Witnesses for the defence were called, who proved that the lady wore frequently certain peculiar bracelets. The prisoner, who seemed stupefied by his emotions, declined to say anything; but his counsel asked the maid-servant, and also the farmer who occasionally sold meat to Orchard Spring, if they should know the rings and bracelets if they saw them.

He then called Richard Perkins, jailor of the county prison, and asked him these questions:

'Had you any prisoner committed about the same time as the prisoner at the bar?'

'I had a man called Haymaking Dick, for horse stealing, the day after the discovery of the murder.'

'Was it a valuable horse?'

'No; it was a mare, blind of one eye, very old, and with a large fen spavin.[59] I knew her well; used to drive her in the gaol cart; but when warm, she was faster than anything about.'

'Do you suppose Hay-making Dick took the mare to sell?'

'Certainly not. She would not fetch a crown, except to those that knew her. No doubt he had been up to some mischief, and wanted to get out of the county, only luckily he rode against the blacksmith that owned the mare and was taken.'

The judge thought these questions irrelevant; but, after some conversation, permitted the examination to go on.

'Has Perkins searched the prisoner, and has he found anything of value?'

The gaoler produced two bracelets, four rings – one a diamond hoop, one a seal ring – and a canvas wheat-bag, containing gold, with several French coins. On one of the bracelets was engraved 'Charles to Laura', and a date. In answer to another question, he had found several severe scratches on Dick's face, made apparently by nails, which he declared had been done in an up and down fight at Broadgreen Fair. Also a severe raw scar on his left temple, as if hair had been pulled out.

At this stage of the proceedings, by order of the judge, the prisoner Dick was brought up. The lock of hair taken by Lord Mardall from the murdered lady's hand was compared with Dick's head. It matched exactly, although Dick's hair had been cut short and washed. Then a Mr Monley gave evidence, that when he met the prisoner, on the night of the murder, immediately after he had left the cottage, there certainly was no blood on his face or dress. The landlord of the Moon Inn was called, and deposed, that he found the corn, placed before the prisoner's horse, uneaten and much stained with blood. On examining the horse's tongue, he saw that it had been half bitten off in the fall the animal had suffered. No doubt the blood had dripped over the young Squire.

It was a bright moonlight night shining in the prisoner's face.

The judge summed up for an acquittal, and the jury gave a verdict of Not Guilty, without leaving the box.

A week after, Haymaking Dick made an attempt to break out of prison, in which he knocked out the brains of a turnkey with his irons. He was tried and condemned for this, and when hope of escape was gone, he called a favourite turnkey to him and said, 'Bill, I killed the Frenchwoman. I knew she always had plenty of money and jewels, and I watched my opportunity to get 'em.'

Thus ends the newspaper report. My uncle died of gout in his stomach on the day of the trial, and died almost insolvent. By Lord Mardall's influence I received an appointment from the East India Company, and afterwards a commission in their irregular service.[60]

THE SCHOLAR'S STORY
[by Elizabeth Gaskell and Reverend William Gaskell]

I perceive a general fear on the part of this pleasant company, that I am going to burst into black-letter,[61] and beguile the time by being as dry as ashes. No, there is no such fear, you can assure me? I am glad to hear it; but I thought there was.

At any rate, both to relieve your minds and to place myself beyond suspicion. I will say at once that my story is a ballad. It was taken down, as I am going to repeat it, seventy-one years ago, by the mother of the person who communicated it to M. Villemarqué when he was making his collection of Breton Ballads.[62] It is slightly confirmed by the chronicles and Ecclesiastical Acts of the time; but no more of them or you really will suspect me. It runs, according to my version, thus.

I

Sole child of her house, a lovely maid,
In the lordly halls of Rohan played.

Played till thirteen, when her sire was bent
To see her wed; and she gave consent.

And many a lord of high degree
Came suing, her chosen knight to be;

But amongst them all there pleased her none
Save the noble Count Mathieu alone;

Lord of the Castle of Trongoli,
A princely knight of Italy.

To him so courteous, true, and brave,
Her heart the maiden freely gave.

Three years since the day they first were wed
In peace and in bliss away had sped,

When tidings came on the winds abroad
That all were to take the cross of God.

Then spake the Count like a noble knight:
'Aye first in birth should be first in fight!

'And, since to this Paynim war[63] I must,
Dear cousin, I leave thee here in trust.

'My wife and my child I leave to thee;
Guard them, good clerk, as thy life for me!'

Early next morn, from his castle gate,
As rode forth the knight in bannered state,

Down the marble steps, all full of fears,
The lady hied[64] her, with moans and tears –

The loving, sweet lady, sobbing wild –
And, laid on her breast, her baby child.

She ran to her lord with breathless speed,
As backward he reined his fiery steed;

She caught and she clasped him round the knee;
She wept, and she prayed him piteously:

'Oh stay with me, stay! my lord, my love!
Go not, I beg, by the saints above;

'Leave me not here alone, I pray,
To weep on your baby's face alway!'

The knight was touched with her sad despair,
And fondly gazed on her face so fair;

And stretched out his hand, and stooping low,
Raised her up straight to his saddle-bow;

And held her pressed to his bosom then,
And kissed her o'er and o'er agen.

'Come, dry these tears, my little Joan;
A single year, it will soon be flown!'

His baby dear in his arms he took,
And looked on him with a proud, fond look:

'My boy, when thou'rt a man,' said he,
'Wilt ride to the wars along with me?'

Then away he spurred across the plain,
And old and young they wept amain;[65]

Both rich and poor, wept every one;
But that same clerk – ah! he wept none.

II

The treacherous clerk, one morning-tide,
With artful speeches the lady plied:

'Lo! ended now is that single year,
And ended too is the war, I hear;

'But yet, thy lord to return to thee,
Would seem in no haste at all to be.

'Now, ask of your heart, my lady dear,
Is there no other might please it here?

'Need wives still keep themselves unwed,
E'en though their husbands should not be dead?'

'Silence! thou wretched clerk!' cried she,
'Thy heart is filled full of sin, I see.

'When my lord returns, if I whisper him,
Thou knows't he'll tear thee limb from limb!'

As soon as the clerk thus answered she
He stole to the kennel secretly.

He called to the hound so swift and true,
The hound that his lord loved best, he knew.

It came to his call – leapt up in play;
One gash in the throat, and dead it lay.

As trickled the blood from out the throat,
He dipped in that red ink and wrote:

A letter he wrote, with a liar's heed,
And sent it straight to the camp with speed.

And these were the words the letter bore:
'Dear Lord, your wife she is fretting sore;

'Fretting and grieving, your wife so dear,
For a sad mischance befallen here.

'Chasing the doe on the mountainside,
Thy beautiful greyhound burst and died.'

The Count so guileless then answer made,
And thus to his faithless cousin said:

'Now, bid my own little wife, I pray,
To fret not for this mischance one day.

'My hound is dead – well! money have I
Another, when I come back, to buy.

'Yet say she'd better not hunt agen,
For hunters are oft but wildish men.'

III

The miscreant clerk once more he came,
As she wept in her bower, to the peerless dame.

'O lady, with weeping night and day,
Your beauty is fading fast away.'

'And what care I though it fading be,
When my own dear lord comes not to me!'

'Thy own dear lord has, I fancy, wed
Another ere this, or else he's dead.

'The Moorish maidens though dark are fair,
And gold in plenty have got to spare;

'The Moorish chiefs on the battle plain
Thousands of valiant as he have slain.

'If he's wed another – Oh curse, not fret;
Or, if he's dead – why, straight forget!'

'If he's wed another I'll die,' she said;
'And I'll die likewise, if he be dead!'

'In case one chances to lose the key,
No need for burning the box, I see.

''Twere wiser, if I might speak my mind,
A new and a better key to find.'

'Now hold, thou wretched clerk, thy tongue,
'Tis foul with lewdness – more rotten than dung.'

As soon as the clerk thus answered she,
He stole to the stable secretly.

He looked at the lord's own favourite steed,
Unmatched for beauty, for strength and speed;

White as an egg, and more smooth to touch,
Light as a bird, and for fire none such;

On nought had she fed, since she was born,
Save fine chopped heath and the best of corn.

Awhile the bonny white mare he eyed,
Then struck his dirk[66] in her velvet side;

And when the bonny white mare lay dead,
Again to the Count he wrote and said:

'Of a fresh mischance I now send word,
But let it not vex thee much, dear lord;

'Hasting back from a revel last night,
My lady rode on thy favourite white –

'So hotly rode, it stumbled and fell,
And broke both legs, as I grieve to tell.'

The Count then answered, 'Ah! woe is me
My bonny white mare no more to see?

'My mare she has killed; my hound killed too;
Good cousin, now give her counsel true.

'Yet scold her not either; but, say from me,
To no more revels at night must she.

'Not horses' legs alone, I fear,
But wifely vows may be broken there!'

IV

The clerk a few days let pass, and then
Back to the charge returned again.

'Lady, now yield, or you die!' said he;
'Choose which you will – choose speedily!'

'Ten thousand deaths would I rather die,
Than shame upon me my God should cry!'

The clerk, when he saw he nought might gain,
No more could his smothered wrath contain;

So soon as those words had left her tongue,
His dagger right at her head he flung.

But swift her white angel, hovering nigh,
Turned it aside as it flashed her by.

The lady straight to her chamber flew,
And bolt and bar behind her drew.

The clerk his dagger snatched up and shook,
And grinned with an angry ban-dog's[67] look.

Down the broad stairs in his rage came he,
Two steps at a time, two steps and three.

Then on to the nurse's room he crept,
Where softly the winsome baby slept –

Softly, and sweetly, and all alone;
One arm from the silken cradle thrown –

One little round arm just o'er it laid,
Folded the other beneath his head;

His little white breast – ah! hush! be still!
Poor mother, go now and weep your fill!

Away to his room the clerk then sped,
And wrote a letter in black and red;

In haste, post-haste, to the Count wrote he:
'There is need, dear lord, sore need of thee!

'Oh speed now, speed, to thy castle back,
For all runs riot, and runs to wrack.

'Thy hound is killed, and thy mare is killed,
But not for these with such grief I'm filled.

'Nor is it for these thou now wilt care;
Thy darling is dead! thy son, thy heir!

'The sow she seized and devoured him all,
While thy wife was dancing at the ball;

'Dancing there with the miller gay,
Her young gallant, as the people say.'

V

That letter came to the valiant knight,
Hastening home from the Paynim fight;

With trumpet sound, from that Eastern strand
Hastening home to his own dear land.

So soon as he read the missive through,
Fearful to see his anger grew.

The scroll in his mailed[68] hand he took,
And crumpled it up with furious look;

To bits with his teeth he tore the sheet,
And spat them out at his horse's feet.

'Now quick to Brittany, quick, my men,
The homes that you love to see agen!

'Thou loitering squire! ride yet more quick,
Or my lance shall teach thee how to prick.

But when he stood at his castle gate,
Three lordly blows he struck it straight;

Three angry blows he struck thereon,
Which made them tremble every one.

The clerk he heard, and down he hied,
And opened at once the portal wide.

'Oh cursed cousin, that this should be!
Did I not trust my wife to thee?'

His spear down the traitor's throat he drove,
Till out at his back the red point clove.

Then up he rushed to the bridal bower,
Where drooped his lady like some pale flower.

And ere she could speak a single word,
She fell at his feet beneath his sword.

VI

'O holy priest! now tell to me
What didst thou up at the castle see?'

'I saw a grief and a terror more
Than ever I saw on earth before.

'I saw a martyr give up her breath,
And her slayer sorrowing e'en to death.'

'O holy priest! now tell to me
What didst thou down at the crossway see?'

'I saw a corpse that all mangled lay,
And the dogs and ravens made their prey.'

'O holy priest! now tell to me
What didst thou next in the churchyard see?'

'By a new-made grave, in soft moonlight,
I saw a fair lady clothed in white;

'Nursing a little child on her knee –
A dark red wound on his breast had he,

'A noble hound lay couched at her right,
A steed at her left of bonniest white;

'The first a gash in its throat had wide,
And this as deep a stab in its side.

'They raised their heads to the lady's knee,
And they licked her soft hands tenderly.

'She gently patted their necks, the while
Smiling, though stilly, a fair sweet smile.

'The child, as it fain its love would speak,
Caressed and fondled its mother's cheek.

'But down went the moon then silently,
And my eyes no more their forms could see;

'But I heard a bird from out the skies
Warbling a song of Paradise!'

NOBODY'S STORY
[by Charles Dickens]

He lived on the bank of a mighty river, broad and deep, which was always silently rolling on to a vast undiscovered ocean. It had rolled on, ever since the world began. It had changed its course sometimes, and turned into new channels, leaving its old ways dry and barren; but it had ever been upon the flow, and ever was to flow until Time should be no more. Against its strong, unfathomable stream, nothing made head. No living creature, no flower, no leaf, no particle of animate or inanimate existence, ever strayed back from the undiscovered ocean. The tide of the river set resistlessly towards it; and the tide never stopped, any more than the earth stops in its circling round the sun.

He lived in a busy place, and he worked very hard to live. He had no hope of ever being rich enough to live a month without hard work, but he was quite content, God knows, to labour with a cheerful will. He was one of an immense family, all of whose sons and daughters gained their daily bread by daily work, prolonged from their rising up betimes until their lying down at night. Beyond this destiny he had no prospect, and he sought none.

There was over-much drumming, trumpeting, and speech-making, in the neighbourhood where he dwelt; but he had nothing to do with that. Such clash and uproar came from the Bigwig family, at the unaccountable proceedings of which race, he marvelled much. They set up the strangest statues, in iron, marble, bronze, and brass, before his door; and darkened his house with the legs and tails of uncouth images of horses. He wondered what it all meant, smiled in a rough good-humoured way he had, and kept at his hard work.

The Bigwig family (composed of all the stateliest people thereabouts, and all the noisiest) had undertaken to save him the trouble of thinking for himself, and to manage him and his affairs. 'Why truly,' said he. 'I have little time upon my hands; and if you will be so good as to take care of me, in return for the money I pay over' – for the Bigwig family were not above his money – 'I shall be relieved and much obliged, considering that you know best.' Hence the drumming, trumpeting, and speechmaking, and the ugly images of horses which he was expected to fall down and worship.

'I don't understand all this,' said he, rubbing his furrowed brow confusedly. 'But it *has* a meaning, maybe, if I could find it out.'

'It means,' returned the Bigwig family, suspecting something of what he said, 'honour and glory in the highest, to the highest merit.'

'Oh!' said he. And he was glad to hear that.

But, when he looked among the images in iron, marble, bronze, and brass, he failed to find a rather meritorious countryman of his, once the son of a Warwickshire wool-dealer,[69] or any single countryman whomsoever of that kind. He could find none of the men whose knowledge had rescued him and his children from terrific and disfiguring disease, whose boldness had raised his forefathers from the condition of serfs, whose wise fancy had opened a new and high existence to the humblest, whose skill had filled the working man's world with accumulated wonders. Whereas, he did find others whom he knew no good of, and even others whom he knew much ill of.

'Humph!' said he. 'I don't quite understand it.'

So, he went home, and sat down by his fireside to get it out of his mind.

Now, his fireside was a bare one, all hemmed in by blackened streets; but it was a precious place to him. The hands of his wife were hardened with toil, and she was old before her time; but she was dear to him. His children, stunted in their growth, bore traces of unwholesome nurture; but they had beauty in his sight. Above all other things, it was an earnest desire of this man's soul that his children should be taught. 'If I am sometimes misled,' said he, 'for want of knowledge, at least let them know better, and avoid my mistakes. If it is hard to me to reap the harvest of pleasure and instruction that is stored in books, let it be easier to them.'

But, the Bigwig family broke out into violent family quarrels concerning what it was lawful to teach to this man's children. Some of the family insisted on such a thing being primary and indispensable above all other things; and other of the family insisted on such another thing being primary and indispensable above all other things; and the Bigwig family, rent into factions, wrote pamphlets, held convocations, delivered charges, orations, and all varieties of discourses; impounded one another in courts Lay and courts Ecclesiastical; threw dirt, exchanged pummellings, and fell together by the ears in unintelligible animosity. Meanwhile, this man, in his short evening snatches at his fireside, saw the demon Ignorance arise there, and take his children to itself. He saw his daughter perverted into a heavy slatternly drudge; he saw his son go moping down the ways of low sensuality, to brutality and crime; he saw the dawning light of intelligence in the eyes of his babies so changing into cunning and suspicion, that he could have rather wished them idiots.

'I don't understand this any the better,' said he; 'but I think it cannot be right. Nay, by the clouded Heaven above me, I protest against this as my wrong!'

Becoming peaceable again (for his passion was usually short-lived, and his nature kind), he looked about him on his Sundays and holidays, and he saw how much monotony and weariness there was, and thence how drunkenness arose with all its train of ruin. Then he appealed to the Bigwig family, and said, 'We are a labouring people, and I have a glimmering suspicion in me that labouring people of whatever condition were made – by a higher intelligence than yours, as I poorly understand it – to be in need of mental refreshment and recreation. See what we fall into, when we rest without it. Come! Amuse me harmlessly, show me something, give me an escape!'[70]

But here the Bigwig family fell into a state of uproar absolutely deafening. When some few voices were faintly heard, proposing to show him the wonders of the world, the greatness of creation, the mighty changes of time, the workings of nature and the beauties of art – to show him these things, that is to say, at any period of his life when he could look upon them – there arose among the Bigwigs such roaring and raving, such pulpiting and petitioning, such maundering[71] and memorialising, such name-calling and dirt throwing, such a shrill wind of parliamentary questioning and feeble replying – where 'I dare not' waited on 'I would'[72] – that the poor fellow stood aghast, staring wildly around.

'Have I provoked all this,' said he, with his hands to his affrighted ears, 'by what was meant to be an innocent request, plainly arising out of my familiar experience, and the common knowledge of all men who choose to open their eyes? I don't understand, and I am not understood. What is to come of such a state of things!'

He was bending over his work, often asking himself the question, when the news began to spread that a pestilence had appeared among the labourers, and was slaying them by thousands. Going forth to look about him, he soon found this to be true. The dying and the dead were mingled in the close and tainted houses among which his life was passed. New poison was distilled into the always murky, always sickening air. The robust and the weak, old age and infancy, the father and the mother, all were stricken down alike.

What means of flight had he? He remained there, where he was, and saw those who were dearest to him die. A kind preacher came to him, and would have said some prayers to soften his heart in his gloom, but he replied:

'O what avails it, missionary, to come to me, a man condemned to residence in this fœtid place, where every sense bestowed upon me for my delight becomes a torment, and where every minute of my numbered days is new mire added to the heap under which I lie oppressed! But, give my first glimpse of Heaven, through a little of its light and air; give me pure water; help me to be clean; lighten this heavy atmosphere and heavy life, in which our spirits sink, and we become the indifferent and callous creatures you too often see us; gently and kindly take the bodies of those who die among us, out of the small room where we grow to be so familiar with the awful change that even *its* sanctity is lost to us; and, Teacher, then I will hear – none know better than you, how willingly – of Him whose thoughts were so much with the poor, and who had compassion for all human sorrow!'

He was at his work again, solitary and sad, when his Master came and stood near to him dressed in black. He, also, had suffered heavily. His young wife, his beautiful and good young wife, was dead; so, too, his only child.

'Master, 'tis hard to bear – I know it – but be comforted. I would give you comfort, if I could.'

The Master thanked him from his heart, but, said he, 'O you labouring men! The calamity began among you. If you had but lived more healthily and decently, I should not be the widowed and bereft mourner that I am this day.'

'Master,' returned the other, shaking his head, 'I have begun to understand a little that most calamities will come from us, as this one did, and that none will stop at our poor doors, until we are united with that great squabbling family yonder, to do the things that are right. We cannot live healthily and decently, unless they who undertook to manage us provide the means. We cannot be instructed, unless they will teach us; we cannot be rationally amused, unless they will amuse us; we cannot but have some false gods of our own, while they set up so many of theirs in all the public places. The evil consequences of imperfect instruction, the evil consequences of pernicious neglect, the evil consequences of unnatural restraint and the denial of humanising enjoyments, will all come from us, and none of them will stop with us. They will spread far and wide. They always do; they always have done – just like the pestilence. I understand so much, I think, at last.'

But the Master said again, 'O you labouring men! How seldom do we ever hear of you, except in connection with some trouble!'

'Master,' he replied, 'I am Nobody, and little likely to be heard of, (nor yet much wanted to be heard of, perhaps) except when there *is* some trouble. But it never begins with me, and it never can end with me. As sure as Death, it comes down to me, and it goes up from me.'

There was so much reason in what he said, that the Bigwig family, getting wind of it, and being horribly frightened by the late desolation, resolved to unite with him to do the things that were right – at all events, so far as the said things were associated with the direct prevention, humanly speaking, of another pestilence. But, as their fear wore off, which it soon began to do, they resumed their falling out among themselves, and did nothing. Consequently the scourge appeared again – low down as before – and spread avengingly upward as before, and carried off vast numbers of the brawlers. But not a man among them ever admitted, if in the least degree he ever perceived, that he had anything to do with it.

So Nobody lived and died in the old, old, old way; and this, in the main, is the whole of Nobody's story.

Had he no name, you ask? Perhaps it was Legion.[73] It matters little what his name was. Let us call him Legion.

If you were ever in the Belgian villages near the field of Waterloo, you will have seen, in some quiet little church, a monument erected by faithful companions in arms to the memory of Colonel A, Major B, Captains C D and E, Lieutenants F and G, Ensigns H I and J, seven non-commissioned officers, and one hundred and thirty rank and file, who fell in the discharge of their duty on the memorable day.[74] The story of Nobody is the story of the rank and file of the earth. They bear their share of the battle; they have their part in the victory; they fall; they leave no name but in the mass. The march of the proudest of us, leads to the dusty way by which they go. O! Let us think of them this year at the Christmas fire, and not forget them when it is burnt out.

THE END OF THE CHRISTMAS NUMBER FOR 1853

NOTES

1. In William Shakespeare's *Julius Caesar* (1599), Brutus and Cassius argue after conspiring to assassinate Caesar in 42 BCE. Having accused Cassius of taking bribes and complaining that Cassius did not send gold when he requested it, Brutus says, 'By heaven, I had rather coin my heart/ And drop my blood for drachmaes than to wring/ From the hard hands of peasants their vile trash/ By any indirection' (IV.iii.72–75).

2. This verse parodies Ann Taylor's (1782–1866) 'My Mother' in *Original Poems for Infant Minds* (1804).

3. The boy taunts Cheeseman by inserting allegations of treachery to exemplify each phrase of the Latin grammar, using the rule itself to insult Cheeseman. Ruth Glancy (*Charles Dickens: The Christmas Stories*, 1996) translates the rule as follows: 'The nominative pronoun is rarely expressed except to convey a distinction or for emphasis, as in you are damned, which means only you and no one else.' Judas is the Biblical figure who betrayed Jesus to the Roman authorities for thirty pieces of silver.

4. A large pantry or side room for storing and preparing cakes, preserves, tea, liquors, or other specialty items.

5. Socially 'cut' or ostracised.

6. Traditional Allhallow's Eve games, many of which relied upon belief in supernatural divination. The customary hope was that the initials of one's lover, or a lover's physical image, would appear.

7. 'Hindoo' was often used, as it is here, as a generalised reference to the peoples of India; Lascars are East Indian sailors.

8. A reference to *The Arabian Nights*, also known as *One Thousand and One Nights*, a popular collection of Arabic tales dating from the eighth century whose imagery, including Arabian gardens, features prominently in Linton's story.

9. This sentence was originally published with the following severe printer's error: 'But one word, one look, from Felix was enough to make me forget every ear nad every prayer of her who, until now, had been my idol and my law.'

10. Henry VIII (1491–1547) ruled England from 1509–47. When the Pope would not grant him a divorce from Catherine of Aragon (1485–1536), who had not birthed a male heir, Henry led the English Protestant Reformation by breaking from the Roman Catholic Church. After the Supremacy Act of 1534, nunneries and similar establishments were dissolved, and those who would not swear allegiance to King Henry and the Anglican Church faced execution. Throughout the following description, Sala puns on the phonetic similarity between Ursine, which refers to anything bear-related, and Ursuline, a Roman Catholic order of women founded in sixteenth-century Italy.

11. Coryphaeus: leader, from the Greek Koryphaios, who spoke for the chorus in ancient dramas; *Bal Masqué* is a masquerade ball.

12. 'Pace' is 'peace' (Italian), indicating that the clerks may only seek peace beside warehoused tarlatan – a stiffened, thin muslin – and barège (so called after the town of Barèges in southern France), a gauzy, silk-blend fabric used for dresses and veils.

13. Puissant is powerful or potent; the Burlington Arcade, opened in 1819, featured upscale personal service and retail shops.

14. A defensive military barricade, often covered with sharp spikes.

15. Donated or charitable.

16. The Royal Exchange.

17. Of Indian origin, a spicy stew whose name means 'pepper water'.

18. Fainting.

19. Gold-bearing.

20. Taverns, usually attached to inns, providing refreshment and/or entertainments for community members and travellers.

21. A tambour frame holds embroidery or other needlework; Poonah painting imitated Asian artistic forms, usually on thin papers; 'kaffir' is a derogatory term for a black African, here specifically a member of the amaZulu people in southern Africa.

22. Pieces of writing in which the first (or last) letters of each line spell out a word or phrase.

23. Laura is the beautiful woman featured in Francesco Petrarch's (1304–74) famous sonnets, and for whom Petrarch held a strong and unrequited love.

24. Youth.

25. A gibbet is a gallows, and Jack Ketch (d.1686) was an infamously brutal executioner under King Charles II (1630–85).

26. A tavern serving 'pots' of ale.

27. A starch taken from the inside of cycad and palm tree trunks, sago was usually prepared by boiling in milk or water.

28. In Worcestershire and the Isle of Wight, respectively, popular destinations for invalids. Malvern was known for its spa waters and Ventnor for its mild climate and seaside air.

29. The back of his head.

30. Prince Azor is the beast figure in *Zémire et Azor* (1771), a French opera based on the *Beauty and the Beast* fairy tale, composed by André Grétry (1741–1813) with libretto by Jean François Marmontel (1723–99).

31. To slaughter completely, from the Old Testament, in which Samson attacked a group of Philistines and 'smote them hip and thigh with great slaughter' (Judges 15:8).

32. Covering.

33. Hawthorn tree branches, which bear white flowers in the spring.

34. An angel of the highest order, usually illustrated with three sets of wings and thought to fly over God's throne (see Isaiah 6:2).

35. Isaac Bickerstaff was a pseudonym used by Jonathan Swift (1667–1745) in *Predictions for the Year 1708*, a hoax almanac targeting the popular astrologer John Partridge (1644–1715). 'Bickerstaff' succeeded in discrediting John Partridge by forecasting his death then insisting upon the accuracy of the prediction despite Partridge's vivacity. When Richard Steele (1672–1729) founded *The Tatler* in 1709, he used the pseudonym and developed the character as the guardian of three nephews, one of whom he makes a courtier; blue garters indicate the Order of the Garder, the most prestigious level of British knighthood.

36. A reference to William Shakespeare's *Macbeth* (1605–06), in which the witches describe the disturbing contents of their cauldron: '…Nose of Turk and Tartar's lips,/ Finger of the birth-strangled babe/ Ditch-deliver'd by a drab,/ Make the gruel thick and slab' (IV.i.29–32).

37. Emperor Caligula, Gaius Julius Caesar Germanicus (12–41 CE), who many claim was mad, reportedly housed his horse, Incitatus, in an ivory stable, laced his feed with gold, and attempted (perhaps in jest) to make the horse a consul and a priest.

38. Towns in South Yorkshire and Suffolk that host some of the oldest thoroughbred horse races in the world.

39. The fork is the front part of a saddle, and Gaskell's invocation of Cesare Borgia's (c.1476–1507) motto 'Aut Caesar, aut nihil' ('Either Caesar or nothing') is meant to suggest that Sir Manley will associate only with respectable horsemen.

40. This identification of Catherine as Squire Hearn's 'only child' is clearly in error, as the paragraph subsequently references 'his son and heir'.

41. A notorious village in southern Scotland where couples eloped due to more permissive Scottish marriage laws.

42. Dissenters chose Protestantism over the Church of England. Mordecai is a Biblical figure who refused to acknowledge the authority of anyone other than King Ahasuerus (see Esther 3:2–8).

43. One who is patient, obedient, and dutiful in the extreme. Griselda appears in Giovanni Boccaccio's (1313–75) *The Decameron* (c.1349–51) and Geoffrey Chaucer's (c.1343–1400) 'The Clerk's Tale' in *The Canterbury Tales* (c.1387). Griselda's sadistic husband repeatedly subjects her to cruel tests of devotion, forcing her to submit to the killing of her children, for instance. The ever-meek Griselda never complains and, as a reward for her obedience, is ultimately reunited with her children, whom the Marquis has secretly sent to live in another land.

44. Dogberry and Verges are the bungling, comic constable and his deputy sidekick in William Shakespeare's *Much Ado about Nothing* (c.1599). The complete plural in this case would be 'Dogberries and Vergeses'.

45. See I Peter 4:8: 'And above all things have fervent charity among yourselves: for charity shall cover the multitude of sins.'

46. Treacle-posset is a drink made with treacle (molasses) and heated milk, plus various combinations of cider, wine, ale, and spices. Philologus (Greek) describes

a lover of letters or 'the word', and Mr Davis uses it here to refer to the author of the article in the *Gentleman's Magazine* for which he was preparing a response when Mr Higgins arrived.

47. The horse's name is taken from a toast offensive to Miss Pratt because she is a Dissenter. The king being cheered is Charles I (1600–49), and the 'Rump' is a derogatory reference to the Long Parliament that executed Charles I in 1649 then declared Oliver Cromwell (1599–1658), who was more sympathetic than the royalists to Dissenters, leader of the English commonwealth.

48. Claude Duval (1643–70), a highwayman famous for robbing stagecoaches and charming women with his fashionable dress and courtly behavior; he was ultimately hanged.

49. Shiny crystallised minerals.

50. A single-masted sailing vessel known for its speed.

51. A group of islands west of Portugal in the North Atlantic.

52. Also 'roistering': blustering, or arrogantly boisterous.

53. A loose, earthy deposit of calcium carbonate and clay (often used to enhance soil quality).

54. Minor properties over which the church holds rights.

55. Hyder Ali (1722–82), a Muslim general who ruled Mysore in southern India and fought against the British, was also the first Indian to lead a corps of soldiers with Europeans in subordinate roles.

56. A large inn, with a courtyard, for the accommodation of caravans in Eastern countries.

57. During the Napoleonic Wars (1792–1815), many British prisoners of war were held at Verdun.

58. Maid (French).

59. Regional use of 'fen' in place of 'bog' to describe a collection of fluid that causes inflammation of a horse's hock joint.

60. Led by the British, these local forces were distinguished from the 'regular' service because they began as volunteer and self-funded units.

61. An early form of type, ornate in style, as opposed to more modern, Roman-style type.

62. The verse is translated from Théodore Hersart de La Villemarqué's (1815–95) *Barzaz-Breiz* (1839), 'Ballads of Brittany', which he claimed was a collection of ancient Breton folk ballads. The extent to which Villemarqué included newer material or supplemented the ancient oral tradition he purported to document remains in dispute. The story here, 'The Clerk of Rohan', tells of Mathieu de Beauvais and his young wife Jeanne de Rohan when Beauvais departs for the crusade of 1239–41.

63. Paynim refers to non-Christians or pagans, as the Count will fight in the crusades.

64. Hastened or sped.

65. Vehemently; forcefully.

66. Dagger (Scottish).

67. From bound-dog or band-dog, a chained guard dog, usually a mastiff.

68. Covered with flexible protective armour, often laced liked a chain or made of small overlapping plates.

69. William Shakespeare (1564–1616).

70. Here, 'Nobody' (and Dickens) opposes the Sunday Observance Bill, an unsuccessful Parliamentary attempt to close pubs, bakeries, theatres, and other recreational venues on Sundays, which, for many in the labouring classes, was the only day they had free for such pursuits.

71. Rambling or drivelling.

72. In William Shakespeare's *Macbeth* (1605–06), Lady Macbeth taunts her husband by asking him if he would '…live a coward in thine own esteem,/ Letting "I dare not" wait upon "I would,"/ Like the poor cat i' th' adage?' (I.vii.42–4).

73. Dickens invokes the Old Testament to suggest that 'Nobody' speaks for many. In Mark 5:9, a man possessed by demons approaches Jesus, and when Jesus asks for his name, the man says, 'My name is Legion: for we are many.' Jesus casts the demons out of the man and into a herd of swine, who promptly drown in the sea.

74. On 18th June, 1815, the Allied armies defeated Napoleon at the Battle of Waterloo in Belgium, ending several years of war.

BIOGRAPHICAL NOTE

Charles Dickens (1812–70), a true celebrity in the Victorian period, remains one of the most well-known British writers. His most popular works, such as *Great Expectations* (1861) and *A Christmas Carol* (1843), continue to be read and adapted worldwide. In addition to fourteen complete novels, Dickens wrote short stories, essays, and plays. He acted on the stage more than once in amateur theatricals of his own production, and at the end of his life gave a series of powerful public readings from his works. Dickens' journalism is a lesser-known yet central aspect of his life and career. In 1850, he founded *Household Words*, where he worked as editor in chief in addition to writing over one hundred pieces himself. After over twenty years of marriage, in 1858, Dickens abruptly separated from his wife Catherine in order to pursue a relationship with Ellen Ternan, a young actress. A dispute with his publishers, one of whom was representing Catherine in the separation negotiations, caused Dickens to engage in court proceedings over the rights to the name *Household Words*. As a result of winning the suit, Dickens folded *Household Words* into a new journal, *All the Year Round*, in 1859, with an increased focus on serialised fiction. From 1850–67, Dickens published a special issue of these journals each December that he called the Christmas number. Collaborative in nature, including the work of up to nine different authors, the Christmas numbers were extremely popular and frequently imitated by other publishers. *Another Round of Stories by the Christmas Fire* is an early example of what would become one of Dickens' most profitable endeavours, for the Christmas numbers often sold over 200,000 copies.

Eliza Lynn Linton's (1822–98) mother died five months after Eliza's birth, and her father was an Anglican clergyman who rejected the notion that girls should be educated. She overcame her unhappy childhood by schooling herself in six languages and reading widely to become a groundbreaking Victorian journalist. Having already published extensively under her own name, Eliza Lynn, when she married William James Linton in 1858, she then appended his surname to her own. In 1848, Lynn became the first woman to be employed as a salaried writer by a periodical: *The Morning Chronicle*. She wrote for over thirty publications, including *The Cornhill*, *The Saturday Review*, *The Literary Gazette*, and Dickens' *Household Words* and *All the Year Round*. Although they did not always agree, Dickens respected her work highly, and she was a close friend of Dickens' sub-editor W.H. Wills (see below) as well as Walter Savage Landor. In 1856, she sold her house, Gad's Hill Place, to Dickens, who had admired the home since he was a boy. A complicated figure, Linton was independent in her own life, challenging many Victorian social mores and ultimately living separately from her husband. She wrote an essay complimentary of Mary Wollstonecraft, yet she was also an outspoken critic of what she called 'emancipated' women and early feminist movements. Linton is well known for 'The Girl of the Period' (1868), an unrelenting attack on the 'New Woman' that appeared in *The Saturday Review*. In addition to journalism, Linton wrote twenty-four novels, including *The Rebel of the Family* (1880), which features one of the first openly lesbian characters in English fiction.

George Augustus Sala (1828–95), a prolific journalist and editor, was one of Dickens' protégés. After working as an illustrator and painter of theatrical sets, Sala turned to journalism in his early twenties. Many contemporaries noted the excellence of his first piece in *Household Words*, 'The Key of the Street' (6th September 1851), and Dickens' approval led to Sala's regular employment as a well-paid contributor. Dickens also edited Sala's pieces so heavily that many have misidentified some of Sala's writing as Dickens' own. Sala wrote for several important Victorian periodicals, including *The Illustrated London News*, to which he submitted the commentary 'Echoes of the Week' from 1862 to 1867. He contributed to *The Daily Telegraph* for nearly three decades and travelled extensively throughout his career to write special interest pieces from Australia, northern Africa, Russia, and the United States. Sala published several collections of his journalism, such as *Twice Around the Clock* (1859), and wrote multiple novels, including *The Seven Sons of Mammon* (1862) and *The Strange Adventures of Captain Dangerous* (1862), which were published in *Temple Bar*, a liberal-leaning and respected periodical of which Sala was the first editor. Sala also co-authored a pornographic novel, *The Mysteries of Verbena House; or, Miss Bellasis Birched for Thieving* (1882). He was married to Harriett Elizabeth Hollingsworth in 1859; she died in 1885, and he married Bessie Stannard in 1890. Despite a successful career, toward the end of Sala's life he faced increasing financial difficulties as he struggled to balance what he referred to as 'bohemian' tastes with fiscal and professional responsibility.

Adelaide Anne Procter (1825–64) was a poet whose work earned admiration throughout Victorian society, from labourers to the middle classes to Queen Victoria. Raised in a literary family, Procter's education at home and at Queen's College prepared her well for a life of letters. Because her father, Bryan Waller Procter (1787–1874), was friends with influential figures, such as William Makepeace Thackeray, Thomas Carlyle, and Dickens, Procter originally submitted her poetry to Dickens using the pseudonym Mary Berwick. She withheld her true identity from Dickens for over a year, and Dickens reflected on his own surprise in an introduction he penned for an 1866 edition of Procter's most famous verse collection, *Legends and Lyrics* (1858–1861). In addition to frequently contributing verse to *Household Words*, Procter published in *The Cornhill* and was active in the Langham Place Circle, a group of progressive women activists. She cultivated close relationships with some leading feminist figures of the day, including Matilda Hays (1820–97) and the American actress Charlotte Cushman (1816–76), who lived in what was then termed a 'female marriage'. Procter agitated for education and employment equity for girls and women, founding the Society for the Promotion of the Employment of Women (SPEW) in 1859 with Jessie Boucherett (1825–1905). Before a protracted battle with tuberculosis ended her life, Procter completed *A Chaplet of Verses* (1862), which she published to assist a refuge for homeless women and children.

Elizabeth Cleghorn Gaskell (1810–65), publishing as 'Mrs Gaskell', was the immensely respected author of several Victorian novels, novellas, and short stories. The daughter of a Unitarian minister, she married the Reverend William Gaskell in 1832, with whom she had several children, two of whom died in infancy. Gaskell's debut novel, *Mary Barton* (1848), took its protagonists from the working classes in Manchester. After reading the copy Gaskell sent him, Dickens wrote to her that the book 'profoundly affected and impressed him'. An ardent admirer from that point forward, Dickens successfully solicited many contributions from her for *Household Words*. In the first issue, her 'Lizzie Leigh' immediately follows Dickens' 'Preliminary Word'. *Cranford*, one of Gaskell's most popular works, was initially published as a series of sketches in *Household Words* from 1852 to 1853. Gaskell is also known for writing the first biography of Charlotte Brontë, with whom she was close friends and a regular correspondent. At the request of Brontë's father, Gaskell completed *The Life of Charlotte Brontë* for publication in 1857, just two years after Brontë's death. After some disagreement over Dickens' manner of dividing *North and South* (1854–55) into weekly instalments, Gaskell continued to contribute small pieces to his journals but chose *The Cornhill* for what she thought of as her best work. At the time of her sudden death in 1865, her novel *Wives and Daughters* was left unfinished in the midst of its serialisation in *The Cornhill*.

Reverend Edmund Saul Dixon (1809–93), rector of Intwood with Kenswich, also published under variations on the pseudonym E.S. (Eugene Sebastian) Delamer. With his wife, he wrote *Wholesome Fare, or The Doctor and the Cook* (1868), 'By Edmund S. and Ellen J. Delamere'. Dixon was an expert on poultry, publishing *Ornamental and Domestic Poultry: Their History and Management* in 1848, an influential text that went into several reprinted editions. He built upon the success of what came to be called 'The Chicken Book' with additional works, such as *The Dovecote and the Aviary* (1851), *Pigeons and Rabbits* (1854) and *Flax and Hemp* (1854). Dixon's pieces for *Household Words* sometimes illustrated his expertise in poultry and horticulture, but also covered other topics, such as 'French National Defences' (1st January 1853) and 'The Ether' (29th May 1858).

William Henry Wills (1810–80) was a vital presence in the world of Victorian letters. An original staff member of the popular comic periodical *Punch*, Wills' early work also included contributions to *The Saturday Magazine* and *Penny Magazine*, and in 1837, the Surrey Theatre produced his play *The Law of the Land*. In 1846, Wills married Janet Chambers, a poet whose brothers published *Chambers's*, a successful Edinburgh journal for which Wills had worked as assistant editor. Mrs Wills acted alongside Dickens in his amateur 1857 staging of *The Frozen Deep*, a drama he produced in collaboration with Wilkie Collins. Beginning in 1850, Wills was an indispensable co-editor (Dickens always called him sub-editor) of *Household Words* and *All the Year Round*, in which he also held significant ownership shares. For an impressive nineteen years, Wills handled the logistics of printing and distribution, oversaw daily office operations, copy-edited, and managed correspondence and payments with all contributors. Wills was the only person Dickens trusted to maintain the desired tone and content for the journal, and he regularly wrote prose and verse pieces himself in addition to editing the work of others. Wills and Dickens were personal as well as professional friends; Wills acted as a liaison between Dickens and Ellen Ternan when Dickens was out of the country, and two men continued their friendship well after Wills left *All the Year Round* due to poor health in 1868.

Samuel Sidney (1813–83) was the permanently adopted pseudonym of Samuel Solomon. After working for a brief time as a solicitor, Sidney turned to the profession of writing and published on a wide array of subjects. *Railways and Agriculture in North Lincolnshire* (1848) and *Rides on Railways* (1851) were followed by a series of pieces on emigration to

Australia, many of which appeared in *Household Words*. His novel *Gallops and Gossips in the Bush of Australia* (1854) was dedicated to Dickens, who praised it. From 1847–57, he was a correspondent for *The Illustrated London News*, and from 1850–51, he acted as an assistant commissioner for the Great Exhibition. In addition to writing a column called 'Horse Chat' for *The Live Stock Journal*, he also managed several horse shows. Sidney collected his extensive knowledge of horse breeding, riding, and management in *The Book of the Horse* (1873), which remained popular for decades.

William Gaskell (1805–84) was a key figure in the development of Unitarianism in the nineteenth century. For fifty-six years, beginning in 1828, he was the minister at Cross Street Chapel in Manchester, and in 1861 he established a weekly newspaper, *The Unitarian Herald*, with John Relly Beard (1800–76), Brooke Herford (1830–1903), and John Wright (1824–1900). Gaskell edited the paper until 1875 and was also a noted lecturer in the Manchester area. In 1846, he accepted a post as professor of English history and literature at Manchester New College; he also lectured at Owens College and the Working Man's College in Manchester. Married in 1832 to Elizabeth Cleghorn Stevenson (above), the couple had several children, two of whom died in infancy. William supported his wife's immensely successful career as a novelist, and the two collaborated on multiple pieces, including 'Sketches among the Poor' for *Blackwood's Magazine* in 1837. The poem, in rhyming couplets, tells of a patient poor woman who is buoyed by memories of her childhood country home, and it illustrates the Gaskells' lifelong concerns about the plight of the labouring and poverty-stricken classes. Through his wife, William Gaskell met Dickens, and two of William's translations in *Household Words* were originally misattributed to Elizabeth. In addition to writing and translating hymns, Gaskell published *Temperance Rhymes* (1839) and *Cottonopolis* (1882), which refers to the massive cotton manufacturing industry in Manchester.

Melisa Klimaszewski is an Assistant Professor at Drake University, where she specialises in Victorian literature, world literature, and critical gender studies. She has published articles on nineteenth-century servants and is now pursuing a book-length project that focuses on Victorian nursemaids and wet nurses. Author of the forthcoming *Brief Lives: Wilkie Collins*, she has edited several of Dickens' collaborative Christmas numbers for Hesperus and is co-author of *Brief Lives: Charles Dickens* (2007).

HESPERUS PRESS CLASSICS

Hesperus Press, as suggested by the Latin motto, is committed to bringing near what is far – far both in space and time. Works written by the greatest authors, and unjustly neglected or simply little known in the English-speaking world, are made accessible through new translations and a completely fresh editorial approach. Through these classic works, the reader is introduced to the greatest writers from all times and all cultures.

For more information on Hesperus Press, please visit our website: **www.hesperuspress.com**

ET REMOTISSIMA PROPE